DEAR AMERICA

The Diary of
Abigail Jane Stewart

The Winter of
Red Snow

KRISTIANA GREGORY

SCHOLASTIC INC. • NEW YORK

The Library of Congress has cataloged the earlier
hardcover edition as follows:
Gregory, Kristiana.
The winter of red snow : the Revolutionary War diary of Abigail Jane Stewart,
Valley Forge, Pennsylvania, 1777–1778 / by Kristiana Gregory.
p. cm. — (Dear America ; 2)
Summary: Eleven-year-old Abigail presents a diary account of life
in Valley Forge from December 1777 to July 1778 as General
Washington prepares his troops to fight the British.
ISBN 0-590-22653-3
1. United States — History — Revolution, 1775–1783 — Juvenile fiction.
[1. Valley Forge (Pa.) — Fiction. 2. United States —
History — Revolution, 1775–1783 — Fiction. 3. Diaries — Fiction.]
I. Title. II. Series.
PZ7.G8619Wi 1996
[Fic] — dc20 95-44052
CIP AC

Trade Paper-Over-Board edition ISBN 978-0-545-23802-1
Reinforced Library edition ISBN 978-0-545-26234-7
B+T 16.99 10/10
10 9 8 7 6 5 4 3 2 1   10 11 12 13 14

The text type was set in ITC Legacy Serif.
The display type was set in Dear Sarah.
Book design by Kevin Callahan

Printed in the U.S.A. 23
This edition first printing, September 2010

For
Tim, Catherine,
and Matthew Walker

Valley Forge, Pennsylvania

1777

December 1, 1777, Monday

It is almost sunrise and we are still waiting for Papa to return. What is taking him so long? Little Sally keeps running out onto the cold step to see down the road, but there is only fog.

We have been up since half-past four this morning, and mine apron is dirty from trying to keep the fire going. Mama's cries are what woke us. Elisabeth and I threw back our quilt and hurried down the stairs so quickly I caught a splinter in my foot.

A tall candle lit the room where Mama lay. Her face was damp. I told her that Papa had taken the wagon and should be back soon with Mrs. Hewes.

"Abby," she said, "this baby shalt not wait for Mrs. Hewes." She squeezed my hand hard, took a deep breath, then let out another cry. I began to cry, too. Poor Mama! Elisabeth put a wet cloth on her forehead and told me to wait by the window with Sally. I do not like waiting.

Finally! We heard horses and Papa's wagon. Sally and I ran out the door waving our arms. "Hurry!" we yelled.

Mrs. Hewes smiled at us when she came into the kitchen. We hung her cloak by the hearth, then followed her like worried ducklings. She was just in time. Mama screamed again, then an instant later there came a sharp little cry.

"Ye have a son," said Mrs. Hewes. Laughing, Papa ran outside and threw his hat to the sky. I could hear his shout echo in the frosty air.

He is happy and wants all of Pennsylvania to know he has a son. But I saw Mama's eyes — she is as worried as I am.

December 3, 1777, Wednesday

The baby is sick. Elisabeth and I have stayed home from school to help.

When I tucked Sally into her trundle last night she threw her arms around my neck sobbing, "Shall this baby die like the others?"

Elisabeth kneeled to kiss Sally, but she, too, began to weep, then so did I.

Mama has birthed nine children: three girls — that's us — and now six boys. We have not had a brother live through his first winter.

After Sally had cried herself to sleep, Elisabeth and I lay in bed whispering. Soon she was quiet. I crept across the cold floor to look out the window. The creek looked like a silver ribbon winding its way among the trees toward the Schuylkill River and the house where Mrs. Hewes lives. Her upstairs window glowed with candlelight and I hoped she was awake, praying for our baby. I was.

December 6, 1777, Saturday

Mr. Walker the carpenter rode up with a new cradle he had made for us. When he asked our baby's name, Papa looked at Mama and she looked at him. Elisabeth and I looked at each other, then at Sally. Our baby was five days old, but we had not named him!

Papa put the cradle by the fire, not too close, but near the stone bench where it is warm. Mama held the baby in her arms for a minute before setting him down in the blankets. She said, "I doth like the name John."

Papa smiled at her. "Yes. John is a good name. John Edward."

So now Elisabeth and Sally and I have a brother. John Edward Stewart. He is so still and so small that when I glanced at the cradle after supper I thought for a moment it was Sally's doll inside.

It is cold at night, especially upstairs with the

door closed. We have moved our bed and trundle next to the chimney for warmth. The string from my nightcap itches my chin, but at least by morning the cap is still on my head and has kept the chill away.

Deer have been coming down from Mount Joy and Mount Misery. Our orchards are full of their droppings, for they come to eat apples left on the ground.

December 7, 1777, Sunday

On our way to church a cold rain began. I was sore pleased Mama stayed home with baby John because of the wind. It blew wet leaves into the wagon and across the muddy road. All trees at Valley Forge are bare except for the evergreens, and there is a crust of ice along the creekbed. Papa said he's happy we are prepared for winter. The barn is stacked high with hay and our animals have cozy beds. The cellar is full of potatoes, onions, carrots and turnips, salted beef, and barrels of cider. We have enough dried cranberries to sell at market.

After prayer meeting we stopped at the Fitzgeralds' to see if Mrs. Fitzgerald needed anything. Her latch string is always out so we shall feel welcome, but I know not why she wants visitors. Her kitchen is untidy. It smells bad and there are mice in her cupboard. I saw them.

Mr. Fitzgerald was taken prisoner at the Battle of Saratoga two months ago and no one knows what the Redcoats have done with him. I puzzle why her boys help her not. They are lazy and quarrelsome, all eight of them. They were throwing mud at each other as we were getting ready to leave, and that bully Tom threw some at my shoes. It splattered my hem. I was so annoyed I walked around the back of the wagon to kick him, but he ran off with his thumbs in his ears and his tongue sticking out. I hate him. He is 11 as I am, but he is just a child.

Reverend Currie and Mr. Walker arrived at our house in time for supper, soaking wet from the rain. Elisabeth draped their coats by the fire (such a stink!) while Sally and I dished out stewed pumpkin. Mama's face went white when they told us the bad news:

The British tried to capture Whitemarsh, but have retreated to Philadelphia, our capital city, and they plan to winter there. We are worried sick.

Auntie Hannie lives there and so do Papa's three brothers and our little cousins. I said we must go right away to rescue them, but Papa said 18 miles is too much mud for our small wagon.

December 10, 1777, Wednesday

Elisabeth stayed home with Mama, so Sally and I walked to school without her. The sky was gray and there was a cold mist. I was pleased to be back and see Molly and Ruth and Naomi again. Before lessons, we were close to the fire drying off when through the window we saw a horseman. The boys ran outside and shouted for news.

"The Redcoats started another skirmish!" came the voice. We all started talking at once and the younger children began to cry with worry. Miss Molly tapped her ruler on the table. She told us to take up our slates and be quiet.

"Quaker families concerneth themselves not with matters of war," she said. Sally was in the front row with the other first graders. She turned around to look at me so I smiled. We are Baptists. Papa will let us be concerned.

December 12, 1777, Friday

Sally's hem caught fire this morning. She was mad because it was my turn to hold Johnny, but she said it was her turn. She pulled on his sleeve and nearly pulled me out of the rocker with him, so I put my foot up against her (not hard) and she fell back. While she was yelling that I kicked her (I did not), her skirt spread out on the hearth and all of a sudden there were flames. I jumped up with Johnny in my arms and stomped fast on her hem. Our screams brought Papa. Now Sally's left leg and ankle are blistered and she's been crying all afternoon it hurts so. I am heartsore and worried. Elisabeth and I made her a cozy bed by Johnny's so she shant have to climb upstairs.

Mrs. Hewes came with her bag of herbs. She also brought corncakes wrapped in cloth, still warm. After she tended Sally's burn, she sat with us to supper. Being a widow lady (she's lost two husbands), her nephew always checks on her and brings news, the latest even more disturbing: General George Washington and his troops are camped just a few miles away at Gulph Mills. Within the week they will march *here*, to Valley Forge, to make winter quarters. This is to keep the British from capturing more of Pennsylvania.

When Mrs. Hewes explained that meant *thousands* of soldiers in our front yard for the whole winter, Mama excused herself from the table and went over to the window. She stared out at the bare fields.

"What shall the Army do for food?" she asked. "Where shall they sleep?"

Sally called from her bed, "They may stay with us, Mama!"

After supper when we were changing into our nightgowns, Beth whispered a secret and made me promise not to tell. She plans to sew a coat and, on the inside collar, embroider her name, *Elisabeth Ann Stewart*, so that the soldier who wears it will remember her and come see her. Many girls have become brides this way, she said.

But I want her not to think about marriage. Even though she's fifteen and pretty, I would miss her too greatly.

I am upstairs writing this at my bench under our window. The candle flickers from cold air coming in, for we lost the shutter in the last storm. Elisabeth is asleep. I can hear Mama's and Papa's voices downstairs. They are worried about the soldiers coming, and about Sally's burned leg. And they worry our tiny John Edward shant live through the winter.

December 14, 1777, Sunday

Johnny fussed all day. He cried so hard he had hiccups. None of us dared to fret aloud, but I saw Papa's face, and Mama's. She nursed him every two hours and this time Sally and I took turns rocking him without a quarrel. When Beth rocked him, she sang in her beautiful voice.

When he's not in someone's arms he is in his warm cradle, and I kneel over him to whisper, "Johnny, thou must live, please."

December 18, 1777, Thursday

I was up early to help Mama with the big kettle, for she is still weak from birthing and it weighs some forty pounds. We put in a salted beef from the cellar and eight onions, then bread on the hearth to bake. Elisabeth and I hurried to the well, but returned slowly so our buckets wouldn't spill. The air was cold and dark and smelled like snow coming.

And by ten in the morning it did come, wet snow

that froze on the fence, but made mud in the road. Our guests arrived by noon: Mrs. Hewes, Mr. and Mrs. Walker and their three little ones, and a neighbour who had lost his wife last month. At the table Papa welcomed everyone while Elisabeth and I helped Mama set the bowls on, then he folded his hands for prayer.

"This day is for Thanksgiving and Praise," he began, all heads bowed. I stood by his chair, one eye open to make sure Sally didn't pick at the pies. He prayed that our Army would be able to keep the British away and he prayed for our health — I knew he was thinking about Johnny but wanted not to say it out loud. "Amen!" came the voices, and quickly the plates were passed around. Congress has set this day — December 18 — as a new tradition for all patriots (that's us) to give thanks to God for the many blessings He hast given America.

December 19, 1777, Friday

I woke to sleet hitting the window and another sound I'd not heard before.

A drumbeat.

Papa came in from milking and said, "The soldiers are coming."

Elisabeth, Sally, and I hurriedly ate our porridge, then wrapped ourselves in our cloaks and scarves. Mama watched from the window as we ran into the road. There on the wind from the south came the drumbeat, several drums now and the high trilling of fifes.

"I want to go see the soldiers," Sally said. But Papa said we must stay by our fence.

"It's too cold," he said, as big flakes of snow began to fall. The fields were turning white and the road looked like frosting with chocolate showing through.

Twice we went inside to warm ourselves, for the wind cut through our clothes. Finally through the gray we saw them. Three officers on horseback led. We ran outside to cheer, but the men were quiet and thin. The sight of them took my breath away.

"They have no shoes," Elisabeth whispered.

We watched for several minutes as they passed by. We were unable to speak.

Their footprints left blood in the snow.

As I write this upstairs, my candle low and our room cold, I think I shall never again complain. For many hours we watched the soldiers march single file into our valley. Hundreds and hundreds were barefoot, the icy mud cutting their feet. Some had rags wrapped around their legs because they had no trousers . . . no trousers, imagine! Mama cried to see their misery. Without thinking, I ran up to a boy — he seemed to be Elisabeth's age — whose arms were bare. I threw my cloak over his shoulders and the look of relief in his eyes is something I shall never forget.

Sally gave her mittens, and Papa wrapped his scarf around the neck of one poor boy playing a fife. As the soldiers passed I saw other families had done the same — if the Quakers had, I know not — but I recognized Mrs. Potter's cloak, her blue one with red trim, and someone had draped a shawl over a small drummer boy. So many were coughing and had runny noses. Elisabeth said, "Can we not please bring some of them in to warm by our fire?"

When we saw the horseman riding back and forth among the men we knew him to be the Commander in Chief, George Washington. His cape fell below his saddle and his tricorn was white from snow. I shall remember him always. He called continually to his soldiers, words of encouragement, and he had a most dignified bearing.

Now as I look down from my window, I see their campfires among the trees, hundreds of tiny lights flickering through Valley Forge. The wind is howling and blowing snow. Those poor men, how shall they sleep in such cold with no shelter?

December 20, 1777, Saturday

It snowed last night.

Sally and I ran and slipped back and forth from the house to the barn to make a path. The snow is almost to my knees. In the barn while Papa milked, I plaited Brownie's tail so it would not swish into Papa's face. I asked Papa why so many soldiers have no shoes and why their clothes are tattered.

"They've been marching for several months, Abigail," he said. "Until the Redcoats return to England our Army shall have no rest."

Since I no longer have my cloak, I wrap myself in a blanket to go outside. Papa took us in the wagon to look across the valley. Some tents were up and there were smoky fires where men huddled. Paths between the tents were streaked red.

Bath night for all, even Johnny. Mama dipped him in the warm water and he let out a wail.

December 21, 1777, Sunday

Church. Mama stayed home to keep Johnny warm. It was dark and snowy out. We passed General Washington's large tent—a marquee, Papa called it. It was pitched under the bare branches of a black gum tree. We were surprised to hear a wonderful chorus of men singing a hymn.

Late afternoon, two officers came to our door and handed Papa a note. It was dated yesterday and signed "G. Washington." Papa read it, folded the paper carefully, and put it in his vest pocket. "I shall do what I can, Lieutenant."

When the men climbed into their saddles, Papa closed the door against the cold and turned to us. "The Commander in Chief needs our help," he said. "He is telling those who live within seventy miles of his Headquarters to thresh one half of our grain by the first day of February and the other half by the first day of March."

Papa looked into the fire, his hand on the mantel. "If we shant obey, the Army quartermaster will seize what we have and pay us only the value of straw, not grain."

December 22, 1777, Monday

Johnny is three weeks old. He is still so tiny the leggings I knit him must be pinned to his shirt so they won't slip off.

Tom Fitzgerald and one of his younger brothers came over. Their mother is in bed with fever. While Mama prepared a basket of ham slices, bread, and cranberries, I gave Tom a hateful stare. His hands were dirty with soot and mud and he wiped his nose with his fingers.

I said to him, "Our cow and five pigs do smell better than thee." Mama turned to me.

"Abigail Stewart," was all she said.

She sent me upstairs for the afternoon, no candle. I held my ink jug to the chimney so the ink would melt and finally I am able to write. There is dim light coming through the window, and though there is snow blowing I can see blurred groups of soldiers. They are in the woods, cutting trees. They are chanting something, but their words are lost in the wind.

At the floor where I'm kneeling, I can see through a crack down to the kitchen. Mama is at the kettle with Johnny in her arm, and Papa is hanging his coat. "The soldiers are building huts," he said. "Their mules are sick so the men themselves are dragging the logs with harnesses."

"What is it they're saying over and over?" asked Mama.

Papa put a log on the fire. He said, "They are crying 'No meat, no meat.' Sarah, our soldiers are starving. Tomorrow, I shall take General Washington some of our grain — two sacks."

December 23, 1777, Tuesday

Mrs. Hewes' nephew brought her over after breakfast to check Sally's burn. "It is scabbing nicely," she said.

I love her visits because she bears such interesting news: General Washington himself came to see her! He wants to rent her house to use as headquarters, because it is close to the main crossroads and is at the junction of Valley Creek and the Schuylkill River. He will pay 100 pounds in Pennsylvania currency. Quite a sum!

So now Mrs. Hewes will move in with the family of her brother-in-law, Colonel William DeWees. "General Washington was extremely polite," she told Mama. "I said I needed a few extra days to pack, but he said he shant mind waiting a week if that's what I needed, being a widow and all. My, what a gentleman, and here we are in the middle of a war with England."

But the General gave her grim news as well: Nearly 3,000 soldiers are unfit for duty because they lack shoes and clothing. Papa explained that means one man in four. They are starving because all they have to eat is firecake, a soggy mess of flour and water; there is not even any salt to cheer them up.

Our poor Army!

December 24, 1777, Wednesday

Christmas Eve. Cold, snowing.

Elisabeth and I made the Egg Nog to set aside for tomorrow's dinner. Mama said it's about time someone in our family wrote down the recipe, so here it is:

One quart milk, one quart cream, one dozen eggs, 12 tablespoons sugar, one pint brandy, half-pint rye whiskey, quarter-pint rum, quarter-pint sherry. Mix. Store by cool window or in cellar.

Mama baked pies — three mince, four pumpkin,

four apple. I whipped cream and eggs for custard. When Mama wasn't looking I licked the spoon, and as I swallowed the delicious sweetness I remembered the soldiers. Were we bad to have so much food when they have so little?

Papa took the wagon to help Mrs. Hewes move her trunks to the DeWeeses' house. Elisabeth and I and the three Potter girls stayed behind to clean the stairs and floors and the brass kettle that hangs from a crane in the fireplace. While we trimmed candles for the lamps, a Negro arrived with a small leather trunk. He took off his tricorn, bowed, then introduced himself as Billy Lee, Mr. George Washington's personal servant. He said, "Thank yous so much, kind ladies."

By one o'clock the General and nine more servants had moved in. They shall be warmer now. It is a fine stone house with a view of the river and a large separate kitchen off the entry. Its root cellar is deep and well-stocked.

It's hard to believe, but already there are huts with smoke drifting out of chimneys. Billy Lee told us the General would not move into a house until his men were sheltered in either tents or cabins.

December 25, 1777, Thursday

Christmas Day.

We could not open the front door because wind had blown snow two feet high. Papa poked a stick out and gradually worked an opening wide enough for him to step out. We measured four new inches along the fence rail.

The Potter family arrived by sleigh, with Mr. and Mrs. Adams and their little boy, who is learning to walk. It was quite a crowd around our table, and loud. Mama roasted four fat geese and two ducks. I found myself with a stomachache from Egg Nog, and feeling sleepy. We opened gifts in front of the fire. When Sally saw the doll I'd made her, she hugged it tight and would not share with the other girls.

(I do not like the scarf Elisabeth knit me — it is brown and itches my neck.)

Johnny was very quiet in his cradle all day.

Reverend Currie was in time for Papa's fiddle and Mr. Adams's tin whistle. The children made so much noise with spoons-on-the-bench (I was serving up pie) that Mama laughed about her Christmas Headache. Before prayers Reverend Currie told us a Negro soldier died in his tent this morning. He was from Guilford, Connecticut, and belonged to one of the captains.

December 26, 1777, Friday

More snow.

Elisabeth spent the day sewing her Bounty Coat. I've decided to make a hunting shirt for one of the drummer boys, I know not who. It shall be safe to embroider my name because they are too young to marry and too young to care.

My thimble fell from my hand and rolled into the fireplace. Sally was quick with the long spoon and scooped it out of the ashes for me.

Papa came in with ice in his hair and beard, but smiling. He said the soldiers — there are at least 12,000 — were served a Christmas dinner yesterday of roast fowl, turnips, and cabbage, plus a swig of rum each. Because Papa is a cobbler, he rode to camp to offer his help. There are soldiers from all thirteen colonies, he said, and all of them need clothes and food; many, many have no shoes or socks.

December 28, 1777, Sunday

It was so cold in church I was grateful Papa brought the tin foot-stove to put under our blankets. I do wish it was proper to build fireplaces in a house of worship.

The snow was blowing so thick we could see our way home only from the dark fence posts.

Bread and sausage for dinner.

December 29, 1777, Monday

Papa took us to the edge of the encampment. Rows of huts make it look like a village. No children are allowed, but I saw some playing near the tents.

"There are nearly 300 women," Papa said. "Some are wives with children, some are sweethearts. But some just like the excitement. Those are women" — Papa could hardly say these words — "of poor reputation."

December 30, 1777, Tuesday

We cannot see out our windows for the ice. It was too windy to go out, so we stayed busy near the fire all day.

Papa is tanning a hide from a neighbour's cow, to make shoes, though he was criticized for helping the Army. Quakers call themselves the Religious Society of Friends, but they will not be friends with General Washington. I understand not why their religion won't let them have anything to do with war.

So far the only families we know who will share their grain with the soldiers are the Walkers, Potters, and Adamses. Mr. Smith will not share any of his wagons — he has eight! — because he does not want the wheels to wear out.

I miss the girls at school (not Miss Molly) and I wish I could talk to Ruth. She has a new baby brother, too, and her older sisters are sewing Bounty Coats, like Elisabeth.

December 31, 1777, Wednesday

The Schuylkill is frozen solid. Several of us slid across with snow up to our knees. We went on purpose to the bend near headquarters hoping to see some soldiers up close. In some places the river is as clear as a window and I looked down to see fish, slow and silent.

Elisabeth and I wandered into the woods to gather pinecones for kindling. As we were filling our aprons we heard a voice. We stopped to listen. Ahead, at the edge of a clearing, was a gray horse with a fine saddle on its back. There beside it was an officer kneeling in the snow, his head bowed, his hands folded in prayer. His breath made frost in the cold air.

Elisabeth whispered, "That doth look like General Washington."

"Yes," I said. It was the same man we'd seen on the road the day the soldiers marched into Valley Forge.

Not wanting to disturb him, we crept away. I felt safer knowing the Commander in Chief of our Army was a man of prayer.

We returned to the ice and to the noise of children playing. When the Fitzgerald boys showed up with slingshots, I took Sally and left with our pinecones. I am unable to be polite when I see them, Tom especially. He threw icicles like little spears at us as we ran. He is a wretched boy.

After supper Billy Lee came to the house. He stood by the door holding his hat, just long enough to tell us Mr. Washington needs to hire a laundress. He will pay forty shillings a month.

January 1, 1778, Thursday

Mama asked me to deliver her letter to Mr. Washington first thing this morning. It was a twenty-minute walk and by the time I arrived the tops of my shoes had filled with snow and I was shivering. While I waited inside by the kitchen step I felt grateful to Elisabeth because she let me wear her cloak. I've decided I like her scarf. I'm sorry I hated it at first and am relieved I didn't tell her so.

The parlour looks different with Mrs. Hewes' cozy things gone. Tables and chairs are arranged in odd places and there are several inkwells with pens (they look to be crow feathers). Green felt tablecloths reach to the bare floor. There is one plaited rug by the hearth where a cat was sleeping. I counted six men in uniform, officers it seemed by their buttons and such, and not one paid me any notice.

Billy Lee came down the stairs and nodded to me.

"Mr. Wash'ton accepts your mother's kind offer. Can you come by this afternoon before one o'clock?"

"Yes," I said.

Now it is past bedtime and I have never felt so tired. Elisabeth is asleep, so is Sally. At noon Papa took us in the little sleigh to pick up two canvas sacks of laundry. We hauled water until my knees bled from the bucket banging them. The big kettle boiled for hours. (We used potato juice for starch.) Mama, Elisabeth, Sally, and I dipped with poles, scrubbed, dipped, then wrung everything out. My hands are raw from lye.

Papa strung rope from pegs across the kitchen and main room, even along the stairway where the heat stays. There are so many shirts, stockings, trousers, and (I try to stare not) private underthings hanging overhead, it feels as if we are in a forest.

Fried beef, ham, and cold apple pie for supper. Tomorrow we shall be able to cook in our kettle again.

Monday is wash day, so we'll do everything over plus Johnny's nappies and our own family's laundry.

Am too tired and too cold to tell more.

January 2, 1778, Friday

At sunrise the mercury said six degrees above zero.

We walked the cold mile to school, but were turned away because it is now a hospital! I tried to peer in.

"Small pox, Miss," the soldier told me. "Now go home, all of ye."

The boys made a carnival out of snowballs and rocks, but the girls and I hurried with Sally to the road. Ruth is cross the army can take over our little schoolhouse whether we like it or not. (I like it, but did not say.) She stomped all the way home.

About yesterday, New Year's Day:

Ten teams of oxen arrived in camp to much noise and surprise. They had come from Philadelphia and were driven by *women*. The wagons were filled with supplies and 2,000 shirts that had been sewn by patriot ladies. Elisabeth said they were Bounty Shirts, but I know not.

The oxen were slaughtered and cooked — their stomach parts were boiled with pepper to make Pepperpot Soup. (Mama calls this tripe, but I call it nasty.) We saw soldiers standing over the fires, using their bayonets as roasting spits. The carcasses are at the edge of camp, and some of the wagons are being broken apart for firewood.

Sally asked Papa, "How shall the women drivers get back to Philadelphia without oxen and without wagons?"

Papa glanced at Mama, then he said, "I know not."

January 3, 1778, Saturday

At six o'clock this morning we were awakened by the sound of drums and fifes. Papa and I hurried out in the blowing snow to see if there was a battle. Other families met us in the road. We expected to see guns ready, but instead saw rows of soldiers, all at attention, at the edge of a snowfield. In front were officers on horseback with the drummer boys and fifers.

In the center one horse was being led out of camp. A man without a saddle was sitting backwards so that he faced the soldiers and General Washington. His coat was turned inside out, his hands were tied behind his back, and he hung his head in shame.

I leaned into Papa's arms for warmth. He told me, "That soldier is being drummed out of the Army."

At supper Mr. Walker stopped in and told us the man stole two hundred dollars from an officer and now his crime and punishment will be published in all the newspapers.

Baths. This week it was my turn to go first.

January 4, 1778, Sunday

A terrible day. On our way home from church we saw a bare oak tree where soldiers were gathered. A hanging had just taken place and the body of the poor man was swinging in the wind. The talk we heard along the road was that he had deserted and been caught running across the iced river. I hate the Army. I wish they'd go home. Sally cried and cried at the sight.

It snowed all day.

January 5, 1778, Monday

Snowed another six inches.

Papa was using the sleigh to haul a dead horse out of camp. (The hide will make some shoes.) This is why Elisabeth and I walked to Headquarters and carried back the laundry. It was so cold, not until we'd been by Mama's fire and kettle for nearly an hour did we finally warm up.

I still have not met General Washington, although I saw the heel of his boot as he rounded up the stairway.

January 6, 1778, Tuesday

Elisabeth and I returned the General's laundry this morning, pressed and folded. There was much busyness. Billy Lee noticed us finally and smiled, taking the bags into his arms and turning for the stairs.

As we were leaving, a soldier came in from the snow with a rush of icy air. He looked not at us, but snapped his heels and saluted to an officer standing by the fire.

"At ease," said the officer. "Spread word that small pox inoculations are to begin immediately, by order of our Commander in Chief."

He explained there soon would be fifty hospitals throughout camp and the countryside. They had started with our little schoolhouse and were going to be taking over some of the barns and meeting houses.

"Abby," said Elisabeth when we were on the path outside, "what if they taketh our church, what shall we do then?"

I know not. Every day there are more things to puzzle over.

January 7, 1778, Wednesday

I am feeling unwell. Papa came in with a hide that smelled so bad it made our eyes sting. He said General Washington has ordered his men to bury the dead horses instead of leaving them where they drop. (They are dying of starvation.) Papa shook his head. "The ground is frozen," he said. "How they shall do this, I wonder. It is difficult enough to dig their necessaries."

January 9, 1778, Friday

The past two days have been above freezing. Snow is melting into mud, making the roads a dreadful mess. Papa's front wheel broke when he tried to haul hay to Potter's. (Mr. Potter helped repair it.) When Papa was returning home he came across another deserter being hanged, a man from Virginia.

Colonel DeWees brought over a cloth full of gingerbread, baked by Mrs. Hewes. He sat down on our bench, to drink Mama's raspberry tea (not English tea) and to complain about the soldiers. He discovered three of them in his barn, stealing hay and lumber. "How shall I feed my horses or mend my roof?" he said, his face in his hands.

January 11, 1778, Sunday

Thankfully our church has not yet been turned into a hospital. It is snowing again.

Johnny is almost six weeks old and has not been out of our warm house. I rock him and kiss his tiny fingers every chance I get. "Please, thou must live, Johnny," I say.

Before dinner I was leaning into the hearth to pull out the corncakes when I looked over at him in his cradle. An amazing thing happened.

Johnny smiled at me.

January 12, 1778, Monday

Laundry. My hands are raw and peeling at the fingertips.

The last few times we've gone to Headquarters, General Washington has been sitting at a table writing letters. I've seen only the side of his face. He wears a pigtail with a black satin ribbon tied on the end. I do not think it's a wig, but his hair is powdered.

January 13, 1778, Tuesday

Today when we returned the laundry, I was astounded to see only General Washington in the parlour, no other officers. I know not where Billy Lee was. The General was sharpening his quill with his penknife. He looked up at us and smiled. His face would have been handsome, I think, if it were not so badly scarred from the Pox.

"Thank you, Abigail. Thank you, Elisabeth," he said. I curtsied, unable to speak. How did he know our names?

He looked at us with kind eyes — they're gray-blue — then he returned to his pen and paper. Mrs. Hewes says Mr. Washington writes at least fifteen letters a day, mostly to Congress. He is pleading for food, clothing, and other supplies, she told us.

January 17, 1778, Saturday

It has snowed for seven days with only wind in between, no stars at night, no moon. I abandoned my journal because I've been ill. I cough until my ribs ache and have been unable to eat much more than broth. Sally said my neck is as thin as a chicken's. I have not had a bath in two weeks.

Two of our pigs are missing. Papa said footprints in the snow were from soldiers. He knew this because of the blood.

January 19, 1778, Monday

Washday. I burned my hand on one of the irons. We keep two in the coals to heat, one in use. I was watching Sally sneak a lick from the molasses jug when I ran the iron off General Washington's collar right over my left hand. It hurts but is only red, not blistered.

January 20, 1778, Tuesday

Sally came screaming that someone ruined her doll. She'd been playing in the barn and left it in the hay overnight, in a safe little house she made. We went to the barn. Someone had slept there and not cleaned up after their necessary. This same person stepped on Sally's doll and tore the dress in half and one arm off.

I can sew it back on for her.

January 22, 1778, Thursday

My cough is better, though I feel weak. Stayed by the fire all day and made onion soup for supper. Mama has asked me to write down instructions — so here they are:

To the small pot I added four large onions (sliced), two quarts milk, two large scoops of butter, salt, and pepper. When it came to a boil I eased the pot to the side of the coals so it would cook slowly until the onions were soft. In my tea cup I beat one egg, spooned a bit of hot soup into it, beat it some more, then poured it back into the pot. Cooked it ten more minutes or so. This we ate with brown bread and baked apples.

Papa is worried soldiers will steal our hens, but the warmest place is in the barn, so we can do nothing to prevent them. He filled a crate with firewood ashes and carried it to the cellar. This is where we're to hide the eggs, small end downwards. To keep them fresh we're to turn them endways once a week.

January 23, 1778, Friday

Sally wanted to bake bread this morning, so I sat in the rocker with Johnny to watch. She tucked her skirt into her leggings to keep the hem from catching fire, then swept a clean spot on the hearth. She took the dough that had risen overnight, set it on the bricks, then covered it with an upside-down kettle, the small one. With the long spoon she scooped hot coals on top and all around.

The aroma for the next hour was wonderful. Sally was so pleased with herself when Mama served it with butter for afternoon tea, that she announced she's ready to get married. We teased about her size (she's just six).

Before bed I brushed her hair into two plaits. She sleeps between Beth and me now because her trundle is cold and lonesome. We are like three cats curled together.

January 24, 1778, Saturday

We woke up to a shock. Our entire north fence is gone, all the rails and posts, all of it. Marks in the snow showed where it had been dragged, piece by piece, toward the encampment.

Papa was so cross his jaw turned stiff. "I am trying to help the Army," he said, "but by God, they are turning my home into firewood." After breakfast he buttoned his coat and said to Mama, "I shall report this to General Washington."

Papa let me ride in the wagon with him (there is not enough snow in the road for sleighs). He took the long way to Headquarters, around the stand of pines, past Slab Tavern, then by Joseph Mann's cabin. Joseph is a freed Negro like Billy Lee. As he lives on Valley Creek near where it meets the Schuylkill River, there were sentries with rifles. They were warming themselves over a small fire.

Two of the soldiers stood in their hats to keep their bare feet off the snow.

At Headquarters we waited outside in the cold. Through one of the windows we could see General Washington and several officers. A prisoner stood in front of them, hands tied behind his back. Soon he was led outside by guards.

"Two hundred fifty lashes for you, mister, ain't enough," said one soldier to the man. "Selling beef to the Redcoats should've got you shot, not whipped, that's my opinion."

Before we could step into the hallway, another prisoner was led out. He was on his way to one hundred lashes for attempted desertion. There were other men inside, handcuffed.

Papa walked to the wagon. "Some other day, Abigail," he said. "These court-martials will take hours."

Mrs. Hewes visited with her youngest nephew, who played marbles by the fire while we had tea. She said that soldiers are deserting nearly every day.

She knows this because some of the court-martials (of those who are caught) take place in the drawing room at her temporary home, the DeWeeses'; also at David Stevens's house where General James Varnum is quartered. (I wonder if Mrs. Stevens does General Varnum's laundry.)

"It's the foreign-born mostly," Mrs. Hewes told us. "They have not the same loyalty as those of us born here on American soil."

January 25, 1778, Sunday

It is warmer, but still we leave Johnny inside. Sally and I stayed home with him so Mama could go to services. I finished mending Sally's doll's dress and sewed its arm back on.

Mr. and Mrs. Smith came to supper. We all have family in Philadelphia and are worried for their safety. Papa and Mr. Smith talked about taking a big wagon while the weather's fair, then returning with as many as will come.

"But Edward," Mama said. "Thee could be shot, mistaken for spies. Please don't go."

"We shall be all right," Papa told her. "Many do it already. You've seen the wives bringing food back and forth, yes? They've not been shot."

They were still talking when we girls took our candle upstairs to bed. I tried to listen, but was too sleepy.

January 26, 1778, Monday

Beefsteak pie for breakfast.

Papa and Mr. Smith have decided to leave in an hour. I am hurriedly writing this because they are choosing two of us to go with them, so that our little cousins will be at ease. I have just heard my name called, and Lucy's, Mr. Smith's daughter. She's fifteen. My dear sister said I may wear her cloak, her beautiful blue cloak. . . . I'm truly going!

January 30, 1778, Friday

Valley Forge. It is late and everyone sleeps. I'm still too stirred up from the past few days and must put it all down before I can rest. I do hope this candle will last — it's as short as my thumb, so I will hurry.

The road to Philadelphia was eighteen miles of mud and ruts that made us turn and bump where we wanted not to. Lucy and I shared a blanket and foot warmer because of the wind. Papa was right. There were many travelers to and from Valley Forge. At the outpost pickets the guards we saw were busy questioning and searching.

It is a crime to sell provisions to the enemy, but people do it anyway because the Redcoats pay in silver coin and gold. The Continental Army pays in paper. Mr. Smith said it is worthless paper, that's why so many civilians are willing to take the risk.

Philadelphia's streets are paved in the middle for carriages, with a footpath of hard brick on each side. Cobblestones are bumpy but much easier on our poor wagon. Everything seemed new and wondrous as I'd not been here since I was small, about Sally's age — Lucy and I stared with delight at houses with lace curtains and painted shutters, outdoor lamps to light the way, and tall carriages drawn by matching horses. There were ladies in fine dresses with velvet cloaks and bonnets.

An assortment of boys, tall and small, hurried along the streets and lanes, carrying boxes. Papa said they were wigmakers' apprentices delivering freshly curled and powdered wigs. "To the arrogant rich," he said, "Philadelphians who'd rather spend money on themselves, than to help our starving soldiers. There should be a law against such vanities in the time of war."

Lucy and I looked at each other. It hardly seemed we were in the middle of a war with enemies everywhere, such was the feeling of gaiety. Shops were open, bells on the doors tinkled when we entered. We purchased nothing, but only wanted to find our uncles (who are also cobblers, one is a silversmith). Auntie Hannie lives with her husband above their little bakery. How happy she was to see us, and she's expecting another baby—I could tell from her full apron.

But when Papa learned she sells bread to the British commander, he was silent. How could she! General William Howe is our enemy. He and his aides are quartered just across the street, down four houses and—Hannie asked us this—would we like to meet him, he's very nice. I thought Papa would collapse with anger.

Candle is going . . .

January 31, 1778, Saturday

It's late again. Busy all day helping Mama with extra laundry from a general whose name I forgot. There are so many shirts hanging — many of Irish linen — we must duck between the rafters.

More to say about Philadelphia: Papa allowed us to stay with Auntie Hannie. The next day, Tuesday I think, he went with Mr. Smith to call on their brothers, while Lucy and I stayed to help Hannie cook and tend her five little ones. But we each did a terrible thing. First, Lucy:

During the babies' naps we went into the tiny shop next door — it is just four feet wide and there is a wood sign above the door that says WIGMAKER. While I was admiring ribbons in his front window, I heard the sound of scissors. Before I could say a word, Lucy had allowed this stranger to cut off her beautiful brown hair! For nine shillings! I could speak not. An English officer might be the next customer!

Lucy is so willful and headstrong she just tied on her bonnet and curtsied. In the street she said to me, "It shall be days before Papa finds out and by then he shall be so pleased to have silver coin it will matter not. Dost thou know that a countrywoman's hair is considered far superior than that of one from the city, Abigail?"

I knew not what to say. I promised not to tell, but I worry that Lucy's pride will get her in trouble some day.

Now, to confess my deed (I see no harm, truly): I delivered rum cakes and strudel to the British general. It was just for fun and to see an Englishman up close, but still I dare not tell Papa.

February 1, 1778, Sunday

Elisabeth finished her coat this morning and very prettily embroidered her name inside the left lapel. My hunting shirt needs repair because I sewed part of the front sleeve to the back sleeve so that no arm can get through.

To continue about last week:

Auntie Hannie gave me a clean starched apron and a basket to hang on my arm. Into it she put two plates of strudel with pecan icing and thirteen rum cakes each the size of my hand — this is her Baker's Dozen, she explained. Auntie Hannie pointed me to the tall brick house down the lane.

I hurried, and rapped the brass knocker three

times. A Negro opened the door and showed me to a parlour where a stout man stood in front of the fire, lighting his pipe. He wore a scarlet waistcoat with a white vest, black knickers, white silk stockings, and pumps with silver buckles. (His knickers were tied at the knee with double bows.) I curtsied, then held out the basket.

He said, "Mrs. Loring, wilt thou see what we have here?"

She was most beautiful with blond hair twisted grandly on her head. Her dress was of peach-colored satin. "It's for tea I'm sure, Billy, come sit." She smiled, then dismissed me with a nod. I backed out of the room as a man entered through another door. He was quite round also, with thick lips, and was addressed as Lord Something-or-Other. His eyes were so pop-eyed he looked as if he had just swallowed a snake.

There were two other men in red waistcoats. They sat in parlour chairs and crossed their legs. All attention was on the tea cart and basket of sweets; no one noticed I was lingering. One of the men — he was plumpest of all — picked up a cake and spread butter on it with his thumb.

Auntie later explained that "Billy" is General Sir

William Howe, England's commander. She blushed to tell me that Mrs. Loring is his mistress. She has disgraced the patriots because she's married to another man, an American officer.

Twice more I delivered cakes and bread to the brick house. The third day Sir Billy wasn't there. He was playing cards at the Indian Queen Cafe, where he often enjoys late suppers.

Now that I'm home again I've decided not to be so angry at our soldiers when they take things from us. Our enemies (20,000, Papa says) are sleeping in warm featherbeds, eating sweets, and playing cards, while General Washington holds his men together with threads.

I've also decided that when the English return to their fat king across the Atlantic I shall confess to Mama and Papa that I served the British commander, but not before. At the moment they are too upset. None of our relatives would leave Philadelphia and none felt ashamed about accepting gold coin from the enemy.

"Business is business," mine uncle said to Papa.

February 2, 1778, Monday

When Beth and I picked up Mr. Washington's laundry, Billy Lee drew us aside.

"Lady Wash'ton is coming from Mount Vernon," he said. "She should be here soon. And Mr. Wash'ton wonders if yous and your kind mother could help upstairs, to make the sitting room — what he says — more suitable. It do need a lady's touch, misses."

When we told this to Mama she sat down, wiping her red hands on her apron. "Whatever do we have to offer the General's Lady?" she said. "She hath culture, and is one of the most wealthiest women in the colonies. Daughters, I need to think. . . . Can ye serve us a nice hot pot of tea?"

February 3, 1778, Tuesday

It is sunny and warm! The path to Headquarters is mud, not snow, and I need not wear my blanket. There is clutter on the second floor, so we arranged the boxes and smaller trunks at one end of the hallway. In what is to be Lady Washington's sitting room (it has a cheerful view of the creek), we brought in a dressing table with a looking glass and Billy Lee showed us where to position the bed. Its four posters at one time had curtains to draw across for warmth, but they're gone now. Mama wants to sew some herself, but our last cloth went for Elisabeth's Bounty Coat and my hunting shirt, which I still have not repaired (and have no desire to).

February 4, 1778, Wednesday

General Washington sent Colonel Meade below Wilmington to meet Mrs. Washington's coach. He worries she's been delayed.

Papa drove Elisabeth to the outer camp to deliver her coat. She told me a soldier on guard duty grabbed it and quickly slipped his thin arms into the sleeves. When he thanked her, she saw he was missing his top teeth and spoke with a coarse accent.

After we climbed the stairs for bed she burst into sobs.

"Oh Abby, I'm so ashamed of myself," she wept, "but I wanted a *handsome* soldier, truly."

I held her hand until she fell asleep. I wanted to comfort her but my thought was that two good things had happened: A cold soldier was made warm. And he thanked her.

February 5, 1778, Thursday

Again woke to drums and fifes. I worry not so much now about the British since I've seen how plump and lazy their officers are, so we took our time eating our morning potato (hot with fried bacon on top).

How shocked we were to see who was being drummed out of the army: a woman! She sat backwards, her legs (thankfully hidden by wide skirts) draped over the horse's flanks. "Who?" we asked among the people gathering at the edge of camp. "Why?"

This is what Reverend Currie told us, for he visited with the poor woman yesterday: Mary Johnson is her name—she was caught trying to tempt our soldiers to ride with her into Philadelphia where they'd have warm beds and plenty of food, courtesy of "Sir Billy." Her sentence: one hundred lashes and drummed out of the Army! I put my hands over my ears because I could bear to hear no more. One hundred lashes on a woman's back . . .

At supper I had no appetite. Papa told us that the women who've been passing freely through the lines of each army now will be stopped. Only generals themselves will issue permits.

"Who knows what damage hath been done, by woman or man?" Papa said. He glanced at me. "Or by child?" I kept my eyes down. Did he know about Lucy's hair, or that I curtsied to the British general?

February 6, 1778, Friday

Still sunny. On the warm side of our house is a patch of dry dirt. I spread a quilt and lay Johnny on his back. He squinted at the sunlight and kicked his legs. I was so happy to see him smile again until Mama came out. "Abigail! He shalt catch cold, he's just a baby . . ." I ran upstairs crying. I only wanted him to feel fresh air on his cheeks.

February 7, 1778, Saturday

Rain all day, winds are high.

Elisabeth and I brought six pumpkins up from the cellar and spent the day slicing them into strips that we hung on string from the rafters to dry (since there are no shirts today). It makes the house look cheerful and there is a sweet scent. The seeds filled the large iron skillet where we roasted them with salt until crisp.

Papa finished four pairs of shoes and took them to camp. He said a lieutenant delivered them to four soldiers who were married yesterday. It seems that some of the women drivers from Philadelphia have found themselves husbands.

Papa also told us another spy was caught. Her name is Ann McIntire.

February 8, 1778, Sunday

Lucy sat in front of me at church and I could not help but stare at the back of her neck. If I hadn't seen with my own eyes the wigmaker's scissors cut off her beautiful hair, I would have known not. Wisps curled from under her bonnet just as before. After the final hymn she turned around, leaned toward me, and whispered so softly I almost didn't hear, "Mama and Papa know naught."

Poor Lucy, carrying such a secret night and day, brushing her hair when no one will see, then quickly tying on her nightcap. She looks sad.

Outside I said to her, "Have you not been eating, Lucy? Your face is so thin."

She glanced at her parents who were over by their wagon then said, "Oh, Abby, the nine shillings are gone." Her eyes filled with tears. "I hid them in the barn under one of the nests. The other morning two hens were missing and all the eggs. And my shillings."

"Are you sure? Have you looked everywhere?"

"Yes . . . yes. Mama's waiting, I must go. Hast thou told anyone, Abby?"

"Not a soul," said I.

February 9, 1778, Monday

It snowed last night and all morning. Mama and I were wringing out the bedclothes to hang when a rumble of horses passed on the road. We ran to the window and scratched off the ice in time to see a sleigh round the bend toward Headquarters.

"That must be Lady Washington," cried Elisabeth, "all the way from Mount Vernon."

"May we go, may we go?" Sally asked.

Mama looked at her hands, red and rough from being in hot water all day. "My goodness, no," she said. "The dear lady shalt need rest from her long journey, not visitors." Mama looked at the hearth, where a fresh round of rye 'n' injun bread was almost done. She smiled. "But mayhaps we should extend our hospitality—" We interrupted her by hurrying into bonnets and cloaks, shoes and wool stockings.

(Elisabeth pinned my blanket over my shoulders.)

The snow was almost to our knees in the field so instead of taking the shortcut, we stayed on the road — a 45-minute walk.

Mrs. Washington's sleigh was by the stone stable, not as grand as we thought it might be and there were icicles hanging from its frame. Suddenly I felt most shy.

Billy Lee opened the door and bade us come in. From the kitchen came several female voices and an excited gasp when we were noticed.

"Who are these dear children?" said one of the women coming over to greet us. She was about my height, extremely plump, and had a friendly, smiling face, though I must admit she was not at all pretty. (I did not like her wide nostrils nor the mole on her cheek.)

"Ma'am," said Billy Lee, "these here are Missus Stewart's girls, those that keeps your husband's shirts, ma'am."

This was Lady Washington!

Sally found her voice first. "Mama says we're to welcome thee to Valley Forge. She hopes the inns you stayed at didn't have bedbugs like The King of Prussia Inn down the road here."

Mrs. Washington laughed. "Sweet child, thank your mother for me. Since you asked, I'll tell. I saw no bugs, but the beds were lumpy and damp for lack of a warm fire. There was quite a lot of noise downstairs in the taverns, but, child, I had nothing but kindness shown me the entire journey, thirteen nights I believe. Roads were rough, of course. We had to leave my coach with the innkeeper near Brandywine Creek because of snow. It is his sleigh outside."

She lifted the cloth to peek at our bread. "Oh, my, can you girls stay for tea? I'm deathly weary, but do need a hot cup, not English tea of course."

We no-thanked her politely and began to back out of the room, but her hand flew up. "Forgive my poor manners. I want to introduce my friends here — their husbands are officers and they've been staying with other families here in Valley Forge. Also . . . Oney, could you come here please?"

Mrs. Washington gestured to a Negro lady unloading food from a large traveling basket. My mouth began to water at the sight of hams and wheels of cheese, dried fruits, jars of preserves, salted fish, walnuts, and almonds.

"How do, Misses?" Oney said, dipping her head slightly.

I noticed General Washington standing in the doorway. (He is so very much taller than his wife, some say six-foot-two.) With hands behind his back he appeared the most relaxed I'd ever seen him. He smiled at us. As Mrs. Washington moved busily around the kitchen, his eyes followed her with tenderness.

February 10, 1778, Tuesday

Laundry done and dried, the bags are too heavy to carry, so Papa put them in the wagon. Elisabeth and I rode on the seat with him to Headquarters. After lifting the sacks down to us, Papa drove off and said for us to walk home within the hour.

Such busy-ness in the front room! General Washington was standing at one of the tables surrounded by an assortment of officers and two of his generals.

Oney was in the kitchen with the cook and two other women. There were eight loaves of round bread on the table — their fresh-baked aroma was wonderful. I peeked in to see a long narrow table against the wall where a soldier-in-apron was chopping turnips and onions. Hanging from an iron hook in the ceiling was a chunk of beef covered with peppercorns. It seemed a fine meal was being prepared to welcome Lady Washington. Oney pointed upstairs, but I heard not what she said because of so many voices talking at once.

Elisabeth and I together carried one laundry sack up the narrow stairway then returned for the other. At least four times we had to step aside to let officers and servants up or down. What a crowded house!

The door to Mrs. Washington's sitting room was ajar. The first time we knocked there came no response. Louder the second time. A woman opened it for us to enter. She, too, was my height and so very plump she had to step back and to the side for us to pass her skirts.

From across the room came Mrs. Washington's voice. She sat by the window to catch the light for her knitting. "Oh, girls, do join us. Let me introduce Lucy Knox" — the smiling one who opened the door — "and these other ladies are friends from Chester County. Come ye in, please."

I again was struck with shyness, but Elisabeth spoke for both of us. "Thank you, ma'am, but Papa says we're to deliver your husband's shirts then return home."

How I wanted to stay! I longed to hear more of their laughter and conversation. The room seemed tiny now with so many women sitting at needlework. Their skirts touched one another's, making it look as if one large quilt were spread over their laps.

"Well, then," said Mrs. Washington, "come again when ye can stay. We could use your help. These poor soldiers are in dreadful need of socks and shirts, so do come back with your needles. Thy Mother is invited as well."

After supper I began the repairs to my hunting shirt, feeling ugly with myself for being so lazy.

February 11, 1778, Wednesday

Finished the shirt. I embroidered my name, not as prettily as Elisabeth's, but it's there: *Abigail Jane Stewart*.

A thaw has made so much mud we did not take the wagon out. Papa told us to stay in, but Sally disobeyed. She ran out into the road and immediately sunk down several inches.

Elisabeth and I stood on a plank to help her. When she lifted her feet out, her shoes were gone.

They are lost in the mud and now she is just like the soldiers.

Papa looked at her muddy legs and said, "Thou shalt stay inside for the rest of the winter, young lady."

Sally cried all morning and would not be comforted by any of us.

"Why can Papa not make me shoes *right now*?" she wailed.

I said, "Sally. You have a warm house and a nice rug under thy feet. The soldiers have none."

February 12, 1778, Thursday

General Washington passed out handbills to all of us in Valley Forge. Too many farmers have been riding into Philadelphia to sell meat, eggs, dried vegetables, and fruits. The General cannot whip them all, says Papa, so he is setting up markets in his encampment — three sites, each open twice a week. This will help feed the Army, though we shall still be paid in paper not silver, and it may stop helping those big-bellied Englishmen.

Papa drove us to the southern edge of camp and pointed out one of the sutlers. This was a small tent with a cooking fire by its door. A man in a fur coat was warming his hands and looking toward camp.

"He's looking for customers," Papa said. "Sutlers follow the Army. They sell liquor, tobacco, and food stuffs to the soldiers, but their prices are high—imagine, two shillings per pound for hard soap. Generals dislike them."

We took cranberries and dried apples to sell at the Stone Chimney Picket. Tomorrow there shall be a market at the Schuylkill River, on the north side of Sullivan's Bridge. Saturday, near the adjutant general's quarters, but I know not where that is.

Coming home, we passed the Fitzgerald house. Six of the brothers were out in the mud playing. There was just a tiny bit of smoke coming from the chimney so we stopped.

Mrs. Fitzgerald sat in her rocker by the hearth, a shawl around her shoulders and two of the biggest cats I've ever seen on her lap. There again in the cupboard I heard scratchings of mice. Even her cats help her not!

Papa split wood, carried in five arms-full, and stoked up her fire. We gave her a sack of dried cranberries, a small ham, and the corncake we'd brought along for our lunch. Mrs. Fitzgerald started to cry when we asked about her husband. There's been no word as to what the Redcoats have done with him.

As I climbed to the wagon seat I looked for Tom to scold him, but he kept a safe distance. We were halfway down their road and he still was making faces at me. If only his papa were here to whip him!

February 13, 1778, Friday

There were many of us down by Sullivan's Bridge to enjoy Market Day and to look at the soldiers. The Schuylkill is still frozen solid and the snow on top is criss-crossed from all the children who slide and stomp across.

Lucy was there with her mother, looking thin and withdrawn. Suddenly there appeared four of the Fitzgerald boys, yelling and banging sticks just to make noise and scare the old people.

Tom ran up to Lucy, reached under her chin, pulled her bonnet string, then ran off hooting and waving it in the air like a kite. Poor Lucy!

The shock on her face — on her *mother's* face —

I cannot put in words. There she stood with her shorn hair for all to see. I hurried to her side untying my own cap, then put it on her head. Tears ran down her cheeks and wet my hand as I tied the string.

"It shall be all right, Lucy," I said.

February 14, 1778, Saturday

Baths. Tonight I washed my hair. As Mama poured cups of warm water over my head, I cried. I'm heartsore for Lucy and know not what her parents will do to her.

February 16, 1778, Monday

As weeks pass, the laundry is looking grayish from our ash soap. Mrs. Washington asked if we could please use bleach.

Mama brought out an old bucket that has been patched many times. She instructed Elisabeth and me to carefully (she would not let Sally do this) bring downstairs our chamber pot, then also the one under hers and Papa's bed.

We poured urine into the bucket, then began

soaking some of the dingiest items, which we later rinsed in fresh water. It is an unpleasant chore, but must be done.

All day it was cold out and overcast. I let Sally wear my shoes for ten minutes so she could step outside. There is a stray cat she wants to pet.

February 17, 1778, Tuesday

Mama came with me and Elisabeth to return the laundry and visit Mrs. Washington. Every day except Sunday officers' wives and ladies from Valley Forge are there in her sitting room or in the kitchen. There's much knitting of socks and mending of shirts and such.

I was so jealous and cross when Mrs. Washington asked Elisabeth to accompany her into camp, to deliver food and comfort to sick soldiers. Why did she not ask me? I wanted to go and think I deserve to go as much as anyone else.

Miss Molly was coming up the path when Mama and I were leaving. She spoke kindly to me, asked about my studies and so forth, but I could not take my eyes off the road — there went Mrs. Washington's wagon with my sister sitting next to her, chatting like old friends! Why am I not as pretty as Elisabeth? I'm greatly upset today.

February 18, 1778, Wednesday

When Elisabeth returned from her day with Mrs. Washington she took straight to bed. Her face was pale and she said she could not think of eating. She rolled onto her side.

"What ails you, Beth?" I asked.

For the longest time she spoke naught. Finally she began to cry. Through sobs all I could understand were the words "those poor soldiers."

February 19, 1778, Thursday

I brought my hunting shirt to Mrs. Washington. "It's quite nice, Abby," she said. "And I know just the boy. Will you come with me tomorrow?"

Will I! I wore Elisabeth's cloak, two pairs of woolen socks, leggings, and my wool skirt. Sally's cap is too small for my head, so Mama gave me hers.

It was windy and gray. A lieutenant drove us past Mount Joy toward the main encampment, past rows of huts, the largest ones belonging to some of the officers. We stopped at the 2nd Pennsylvania Brigade, commanded by General Wayne, and stepped down into mud. There was a stench coming from between huts and I knew why the instant I saw yellow snow and human waste. (Such a filthy habit!)

If Mrs. Washington noticed, she said naught. I followed her into the hut. We both bent over to avoid hitting our heads. It was dark therein, and so smoky my eyes immediately began to sting. The fireplace had a small iron kettle sitting on stones, but the wood was either wet or green so it gave off no warmth. In a corner lay a pile of beef bones from an earlier meal.

Each side of the small cabin had narrow bunks, stacked three high. On a lower one lay a soldier with no blanket, just bits of hay sprinkled over him for warmth. His bare feet stuck out at the end of his bed. His toes were black, the soles of his feet dark green, and there was a smell of rotten meat coming from them. I pressed my hand to my mouth.

A young girl sat next to him on her little travel bag, weeping.

"Mrs. Kern?" said Mrs. Washington. "May I offer you prayer? The surgeon will take thine husband shortly."

"Yes, ma'am, please." The girl could not control her weeping and I found myself crying, too. Following Mrs. Washington's example I knelt in the cold dirt. The poor soldier was shivering as she took his hand in hers.

"Dear Lord," she began, "please comfort this good man and his wife, be with them . . ."

She embraced Mrs. Kern (a girl near Elisabeth's age). Just then we saw a shadow of men outside and a stretcher.

My candle is hissing . . .

February 20, 1778, Friday

Again gray and cold. To finish about yesterday:

Mrs. Washington and I visited eight huts. Each time, she talked with the soldier, asked about his family, then knelt in prayer for him. If she was tired (or as cold as I was) she uttered not one complaint.

Near two o'clock in the afternoon we came to a tent at the edge of camp. Outside a woman bent over a kettle of wash. Rags were wrapped around her feet. Mrs. Washington smiled at her.

"Good day, madam," she said. "I'd like to

introduce Miss Abigail Stewart. She's made a shirt I think will fit your boy nicely."

"He's yonder, m'lady. Can y'hear the fifes and drums over the next hill? Such a racket all day long. But I will give him thy shirt, Miss," she said to me, "soon as he returns. God bless ye."

As we rode back toward Headquarters I stared at the outer tents, small and shabby most of them. There were laundry kettles, and clotheslines were strung between branches. Mrs. Washington said drummer boys are paid seven and one-third dollars per month, and some are so young their mothers camp nearby to care for them. She pulled her cloak up to her chin and turned stiffly to smile at me.

"The women offer much help to the brigades," she said. "But once the Army is on the march again, going toward battle or from it, my husband says camp followers are a nuisance."

The wind was cutting through my clothes when we neared the schoolhouse which, of course, was now a hospital. I was beginning to shiver after so many hours outdoors. My stomach felt hollow with hunger, for I'd eaten just two biscuits for break-fast and Mrs. Washington's food basket was now empty.

Several dogs were slinking about, trying to get near a trough that was below the window. A soldier jabbed at them with his bayonet, but as he had no shoes he remained standing on his hat and gave no chase. One dog lunged for the trough and ran off with what looked like a piece of wood in its mouth. Another did the same.

Our wagon driver pulled the reins to stop, but we did not get down. A man's scream from inside the schoolhouse was so horrible, so full of begging and pain, I looked at Mrs. Washington with tears in my eyes.

"What's happening?" I asked.

She, too, could not hold back tears. "I'm afraid, my dear, the surgeon is at work."

I then realized the trough was overflowing, not with firewood, but with human hands and feet.

February 21, 1778, Saturday

I have felt heartsore all day. When I told Mama about the soldiers, I buried my head in her lap and cried. Elisabeth also came to the hearth.

"They're dying from the Pox," she told us, trying to hold back tears, "and the Putrid Fevers. Mama . . .

I watched a surgeon saw off a man's leg, right before mine eyes." Elisabeth now could not stop weeping. Mama stroked her hair.

Finally Elisabeth dried her face with her apron. "The poor soldier had a bullet clenched between his teeth to keep from screaming, but so great was his pain . . . oh, Mama . . . when he did open his mouth to cry out, the bullet dropped back into his throat. While he was choking the surgeon kept sawing . . . and he died right there."

"Dear . . . dear . . ." said Mama.

Sally sat next to us, nervously rocking Johnny's cradle. "Why must his leg be cut off?" she asked.

Papa's voice came from the doorway. "Because the soldiers have no shoes, the snow freezes their feet."

We waited for him to say more.

"Is it like the frost that kills Mama's roses?" asked Sally.

"Yes," Papa said. "But a soldier whose hand or foot freezes must have it removed if it turns black, otherwise the black turns to green. Green means infection."

Papa took his coat off the peg and looked at us for a moment. His voice was soft.

"The only way to get rid of such an infection is

to cut it off. I'm sorry, daughters, that ye had to see such suffering."

It is late now. Mama is downstairs rocking Johnny, and I can hear Papa's snoring. Just before our noon meal, Oney knocked on our door, asking if we'd help her find some eggs.

"How many do you need, Oney?" Mama asked.

"Forty, ma'am."

"Forty?"

"Yes, ma'am. Lady Washington is baking a cake for her husband as tomorrow is his birthday, his forty-sixth birthday. Her recipe calls for forty eggs."

Elisabeth and I spent the afternoon calling on neighbours while Papa waited in the wagon with our crate of wood ashes. We had thirteen eggs ourselves, though small ones from our pullets. Mrs. Smith gave seven, and as we left I glanced up at the window by their chimney. There was Lucy, looking out, but she moved away from the glass so quickly I had trouble believing what I'd seen: her head was shaved.

By three o'clock we delivered 42 eggs to Mrs. Washington's kitchen. She herself did not receive us, because she, the General, and several officers and their wives had just begun their evening meal. Oney said this way they'll finish eating before they need to use candlelight.

February 22, 1778, Sunday

Windy and dark all day. Worship seemed longer than usual. I saw Lucy's two sisters and their parents in the front pew, but no Lucy. They've punished her by shaving her head and, to shame her, will not let her wear a bonnet. How I grieve for her, poor Lucy.

Though the ride home was bitter cold, I was cheered by the distant sound of singing among the brigades. Papa said General Washington encourages his troops to attend divine services every Sunday and to pray daily. He also said this:

"To the distinguished character of soldier and patriot, it should be our highest glory to add the more distinguished character of Christian."

It was most comforting to hear choruses of hymns on such a bleak day.

After sundown, the festive music from a band brought us, with shawls quickly wrapped over shoulders, from our hearth out onto our step. The air was icy and the road dark, but we could see torches of neighbours coming on foot to Headquarters. Papa let us girls hurry along the road with him—I was out of breath and my cheeks were numb when we arrived.

An artillery band was serenading General Washington!

Mrs. Washington stepped outside, clapping her hands with pleasure. "Thank you, thank you!" she called to the cold men. "How I love the sound of fifes and drums, such a fine way to honour his birthday. The General and I thank ye." She took fifteen shillings out of a tiny silk purse tied to her waist and paid the bandleader.

When she invited the musicians in, those of us watching turned for home. How they all fit in that snug house, I know not, because soon there was dancing. Through the window I saw the General with his hands on his hips and his pigtail bouncing—he was doing a jig!

February 23, 1778, Monday
When Elisabeth and I picked up the laundry at Headquarters, Mrs. Washington invited us into the

warm kitchen. There on a pewter plate were two slivers of cake.

"I saved these for you, girls, some of the Old Man's birthday cake. Here ye go."

It had been many weeks since either of us had eaten anything so delicious. I tried to be polite, but forgot my mouth was full when I asked for her recipe, and crumbs spit out over my apron. Elisabeth scolded me with her eyes, but if Mrs. Washington noticed my bad manners she said naught.

From her husband's desk she took up a fresh piece of paper, dipped his quill in ink, and wrote down the recipe (which I shall keep between pages of this journal instead of copying it all down). I remember the ingredients, but not how it's put together:

40 eggs
4 pounds butter
4 pounds sugar powdered
5 pounds flour
5 pounds fruit
mace & nutmeg
wine & some fresh brandy

Mama hugged us and laughed. "It's good ye were

able to taste such a fine cake," she said, "because the day we have forty eggs and four pounds of sugar to spare will be the day I grow wings."

The wind beat against the house all day so that we felt it blow in through cracks and under the door. Only the fire and hot kettle of wash kept us warm.

A great noise of horses and wagons passed by on the way to Headquarters, but we were unable to see out the steamy windows. Sally demanded I let her wear my shoes outside so she could watch the visitors, but when I refused she smacked our long spoon against the stones until it splintered in half. She stuck her jaw out and was not at all sorry for her temper. I was sore pleased when Mama put her in the corner with a swat.

Johnny is looking a bit more rosy in the cheeks. We lay him on the plaited rug, on his stomach, and after several minutes of wiggling he rolled over onto his back with a thump. He was so surprised he let out a howl and would not stop until I picked him up.

Sally sulked all day!

February 24, 1778, Tuesday

Elisabeth and I saw the new person standing by General Washington's fireplace. His name is Baron von Steuben and he is as stout and ugly as a nose.

At his side was a dog, a greyhound, with a thin blue collar. His name is Azor and a more well-mannered dog I've never seen, because when General Washington offered him a cracker he politely lifted his paw, put it on the General's knee, then daintily took a bite. Azor holds his head high, as if posing for a portrait. I should like to play fetch with him.

As we carried the laundry downstairs Billy Lee told us that when Benjamin Franklin was in Paris he met von Steuben and asked him to sail to America to help train our soldiers. He is an Army officer from Prussia and speaks no English, but brought an interpreter with him, a young Frenchman.

"There . . . see that boy by the window?" pointed Billy Lee. "His name is Pierre—"

We heard no more because I, and especially Elisabeth, could not take our eyes off the boy. He was perhaps seventeen years of age, and was striking in his looks, dark hair swept back into a queue with a ribbon that matched his red waistcoat. His white pants were tucked into tall black riding boots, and he was trim.

He was speaking in French to one of the aides, Mr. Alexander Hamilton. They both laughed, then continued a lively exchange.

"Misses?" Billy Lee said to us, gently trying to usher us to the door. I did not want to leave, nor did Elisabeth, but leave we did.

A wagon outside was being prepared to take the Baron and his charming interpreter to their quarters, Slab Tavern. With them would go their private chef and valet. And, of course, Azor.

This is what Elisabeth said on our way home: "I think I shall begin sewing right away."

"What shall you sew?" I asked.

"Pierre needs a good American coat," she answered.

I knew Elisabeth. She did not get what she wanted with her first Bounty Coat so she was going to try again. But she must have forgotten one thing: We have no cloth.

February 25, 1778, Wednesday

Elisabeth had not forgotten we have no cloth.

Without asking Mama or saying anything to me,

she went upstairs and took apart her cloak seam-by-seam (this I found out later). Now neither of us has anything warm to wear over our dresses — I hate her! She cares not for anyone but herself.

Worst of all is she did this secretly, pretending the reason she wanted not to go outside was because she didn't feel well. When I asked if I could wear her cloak, she said no, that she had snagged it on the fence and was mending the sleeve. She lied. And I believed her.

So when we went to Slab Tavern with only shawls to warm us, I thought nothing of it. We had a basket of corncakes Mama baked for the Baron, and for some reason I did not question Elisabeth about the package in her arms wrapped with string.

Slab Tavern is called such because of the large stone slab below the door. A wood sign above shows a horseman at full gallop. From here it is a short walk to Headquarters, but first you must cross the creek and pass Joseph Mann's cabin.

Inside were smoke and loud voices. Azor lay by the hearth lapping up a bowl of toddy. Von Steuben sat nearby with his pipe. His valet stood behind him, plaiting his pigtail. They looked not at us until we stood inches in front of them.

We curtsied and held out the corncakes. The Baron said something we understood not, then turned to his assistant. "Vogel," he called. Then Vogel said to us, "Little ladies, Lieutenant General Baron Friedrich Wilhelm Ludoff Gerhard Augustin von Steuben says thank ye. Now good-bye."

Elisabeth curtsied again and quickly held out her package.

"This is a gift for Pierre," she said, "from an American admirer. My name is inside on the collar, sir, please tell him." She backed away, tugging at my arm for I stood speechless, finally understanding what she'd done with her beautiful blue cloak.

February 26, 1778, Thursday

I have not spoken to Elisabeth since yesterday morning. I am too cross even to tell Mama what she has done.

Sleet and wind all day. We stayed in. For dessert after supper we roasted hickory nuts in Mama's long pan.

February 27, 1778, Friday

A great miracle has happened in Valley Forge.

We heard shouts early this morning and saw many neighbours running and driving their wagons toward the Schuylkill. Two miles above Headquarters at Pawling's Ford we saw nearly 100 cavalrymen riding into the icy water.

"The shad are running!" came the cry.

"Shad?" Papa said in amazement. "This time of year?"

We stood near Perkiomen Creek, where it flowed toward the Schuylkill, and watched. The soldiers formed a line across the river, wading their horses upstream while beating the surface with branches.

How cold their fingers must be! thought I.

Those standing in the shallows threw nets and pulled in shad by the thousands. These men were shaking with cold and their hands and lips were blue, but they kept working.

Finally an officer started a victory chant and soon all were out of the river and drying off with blankets brought by some of us. Along the banks many soldiers dropped to their knees in exhaustion, I thought, but soon I realized they were praying.

"Why?" I asked Papa.

He looked down at me and drew me into his warm arms. "Why? The famine is over, Abigail. Their prayers and mine have been answered. A river overflowing with fish in the middle of winter? It has not happened in thy lifetime, nor mine. Only Almighty God could arrange such a miracle, my daughter, and these good men are thanking Him."

A horseman caught up with us on the road back from the river and tossed a wet sack of fish into the back of our wagon.

"For thy family, Mr. Stewart," he called, and was off.

Papa waved his mittened hand and took up the reins. His beard was covered with frost, but still I saw his smile.

Mama baked the shad in vinegar then rolled up each piece. Sisters and I helped her tuck them into jars. Into each we poured vinegar and onions to pickle, then held dripping candles over them to seal. Our house stinks, but the pantry is full again.

February 28, 1778, Saturday

Sally lost her two top teeth, one early this morning when she bit into a biscuit, the other after she wiggled it for several hours. She kept sticking out her tongue through the space and making baby sounds, so I gave her my shoes to wear. Now she is in the barn playing with her doll and not bothering me any more.

Any time of day or night we hear drummers and fifers practicing. Papa calls it a "confusing noise" that disrupts the peace of our valley. Myself, it is the shots of muskets and cannons I most dislike.

March 1, 1778, Sunday

Johnny is three months old today. He is chubby! We made pretzels as big as Papa's hand by rolling dough into strips, then bending each one as if they were arms crossed onto shoulders. We pressed salt on top then baked them on the bricks. When they were done, Johnny held one in his little hand and chewed on it with his gums, for he has no teeth.

It snowed heavy all day. We could not see out the windows, so made do with firelight until bed. No church.

March 2, 1778, Monday

Still snowing.

I made up with Elisabeth. It is very near impossible to stay mad at someone you must look at hour after hour. Besides we had to make our way together through the storm to Headquarters. We took the little sleigh by ourselves, our old mare Buttercup pulling.

General Washington was sitting by the fire in a ladder-back chair. Nearby, trying to use light from the snowy window, sat an artist at his easel. He was sketching with charcoal a portrait of the General.

Mrs. Washington slipped us each a small square of gingerbread when we passed the kitchen. "That's Charles Willson Peale," she told us. "He painted the General a few years ago after the French and Indian War, and he plans to do the other generals here. He's a captain with the Pennsylvania brigade."

I knew he was a soldier because his toes were sticking out of his shoes.

March 3, 1778, Tuesday

Snowed all night. At seven this morning the wind stopped. We looked out to see a pink sunrise, but in the north were black clouds moving swiftly our way. Papa said to hurry, return the laundry to Headquarters before the storm arrived.

Billy Lee waved at us from the kitchen where he was pouring boiling water into teapots. Several officers in the front room talked in low voices as I hurried upstairs to knock on Mrs. Washington's door.

Thinking I heard an answer, I turned the knob and stepped in. A small fire blazed in the grate. She looked up from her desk under the window. A pair of spectacles was on her nose, and opened in front of her was a Bible.

"Ma'am, I'm sorry," said I, realizing she wished to be left alone.

"Quite all right, dear," she said, then turned back to her desk. At that moment Oney rushed in with apologies to her mistress and a hand on my elbow to usher me out.

"Shame!" she scolded me. "Lady Wash'ton is not to be disturbed at this hour. She has devotions every morning from eight 'til nine."

"I'm sorry, Oney."

"Hush, chile, don't cry. Billy Lee say he gots gingersnaps for you and sister, so come on now."

I felt miserable. To be scolded in front of Mrs.

Washington was something I'd not intended and though I managed not to bawl, my eyes filled with tears. Elisabeth and I stood in the kitchen to warm up and eat a cookie before the ride home. I heard boots in the hallway and men's voices, so I tried quickly to wipe my cheeks dry.

Someone came beside me, offering a laced handkerchief. I looked up into the blue eyes of Pierre. He spoke in French, then when I didn't respond, he said with a heavy accent, "Are you sad, pretty one?"

I said naught, only stared at him, wanting to hear more of his speech, so dear was his accent. Behind him stood Elisabeth. When I saw her mad face, I curtsied and immediately helped her carry the last bag to our sleigh.

We said nothing to each other the way home. I unhitched Buttercup and led her into the barn while Elisabeth dragged the sacks to our door. It was beginning to snow. When she looked at me I realized her chin was quivering.

"Abby," she said, struggling not to cry, "Pierre wasn't wearing my coat."

March 4, 1778, Wednesday

I have been trying hard to be nice to Elisabeth, for she breaks into tears every time I mention Pierre.

Mama isn't cross about the cloak, but she was most upset that Beth told so many lies.

"Elisabeth Ann," she said, "no matter how good thy deed may be, if thou art dishonest along the way that good deed will always be tainted."

Elisabeth was silent when we went to bed. She stared at the ceiling until Sally fell asleep then looked over at me by the window. I have a new candle so there's no worry of it going out tonight.

"Pierre is handsome and clever, yes, Abby?"

Yes, I nod. I'm trying to write.

"Suppose he stays in America after the war," she says. "He shalt need a bride, will he not? What dost thou think he's done with my coat? Answer me, Abigail."

"Well," say I, "mayhaps Pierre gave thy coat to a soldier who did not have one—that's possible. And about being a bride, thou art nice enough and pretty enough to marry anyone you please, Beth."

She is still awake *and* talking so I shall write this quickly before she asks me another question. Today Mr. Walker came by the barn while Papa was repairing one of the pens. I heard him say that a friend who lives west of Valley Creek was caught sneaking information to the British and he's going to be hanged tomorrow. Hanged! — one of our own neighbours! His poor family.

The other thing I learned is that a soldier I visited, the one who had his feet amputated, has died from fever. His wife, Mrs. Kern, would not leave his side and had to be carried away in a faint. She has no family now, no place to go. The Army says if she does not find another soldier to marry within three weeks she must leave the encampment.

I'm so sad for her. Tomorrow I shall ask if she can stay with us.

March 5, 1778, Thursday

It is very cold and windy. Mercury: 12 degrees.

Sally likes to help Papa with the milking. He carries her from the house to the hay so she shant get her stockings wet. When I saw her plaiting Brownie's tail, I laughed out loud. It reminded me of Vogel plaiting Baron von Steuben's pigtail, though I shall admit the Baron is a sight more handsome than Brownie's rump.

We spent the afternoon riding the edge of the encampment, asking for Mrs. Kern and asking the Army chaplains if there had been any weddings. Two, but none with Mrs. Kern.

Finally Papa drove south by Trout Creek. Here the tents were low and shabby. A woman came out to stare. She wore a cape over a ragged dress and her feet were muddy. She pointed down the row.

Papa drove on, calling for Mrs. Kern. The last tent had a small fire in front where a woman warmed her hands. Papa stepped down and told us to wait. He ducked into the tent and a moment later carried out in his arms a limp Mrs. Kern. We helped her settle into hay in the back of our wagon, Elisabeth and I on either side to warm her.

It's late now. We have made a cot by our bed upstairs for our new guest. She told us her name is Helen and that she is sixteen years of age. She fell instantly asleep and when Beth and I covered her with our quilt we noticed that Helen is soon to have a baby.

March 6, 1778, Friday

Sally and I had such a quarrel this morning that Mama put us in separate corners. I was most miserable and mad and embarrassed that our guest heard me crying.

When Ruth and Naomi came to call and invited me to slide on the river, I was bitterly angry to have to stay inside. It was a pretty day, no clouds.

But just before noon, when Mama was setting bread on the table, Reverend Currie and two men knocked hard on our door, calling for Papa.

"Hurry!" they cried, and Papa was off. Upon hearing their news Mama slumped at the table and lay her head in her arms.

"What, what?" we asked. Finally, the terrible words: "Some children have fallen through the ice."

I ran outside without my shawl. I ran to Headquarters and past. There in the ice, like a broken window, was a large hole. A crowd waited on the banks in the cold shade. Two soldiers stood wet and shivering, others shouted to one another. When I saw Naomi and Ruth huddled together I ran to them. They were dripping.

"Abby," they cried, "the boys are gone."

"What boys?"

"The Fitzgeralds, five of them, gone. They were chasing us and we heard a shot. We knew not until too late that it was ice cracking. It was shallow where we fell through, but, oh . . ." They embraced each other, weeping loudly.

It is half-past nine o'clock and my candle is short. Mama went with Mrs. Potter, Mrs. Adams, and the other ladies to comfort Mrs. Fitzgerald. I shall never see Tom again. I am sorry I hated him so.

March 8, 1778, Sunday

It rained all day. The air is warmer.

Some soldiers from the Vermont brigade were patrolling the lower end of the river. They found the bodies of Tom, Nate, Phillip, Howard, and Sammy near a beaver dam. I am so very sad for their mother and their three littlest brothers.

Helen Kern has brought much help to our chores of laundry and ironing. She made friends with Sally by sewing a tiny lace shawl for her doll. Helen is cheerful, but at night when the house is quiet I hear her crying under her pillow.

March 14, 1778, Saturday

The dark woods look green! There are buds in the orchard, on our apple trees.

Sisters, Helen, and I ran into the road without shoes. We ran across the fields. Our feet were cold, but it felt wonderful to have soft dirt in our toes. We ran to the crest of the hill and looked down into the valley below Mr. Stevens's house, where General Varnum is quartered.

There in rows and rows were soldiers drilling, marching, saluting, and loading muskets. Many were barefoot like us, but there were many in new uniforms, snappy blue jackets with buttons, white pants, tricorns. It was a sight!

We hurried as close as we could without being seen, and hid under some dogwood bushes still bare. Baron von Steuben paced in front of the men, shouting orders in several different languages — not one of them did we understand. There were three men with him interpreting. One listened to the Baron's commands, turned to Pierre, translated them into German, then Pierre turned to Alexander Hamilton with French words, which Mr. Hamilton then shouted into English. Only then did the soldiers respond to the "Left drill!" "Right drill!" or whichever it was.

Several times we heard Mr. Hamilton shout curse words, then shrug with embarrassment because that was what had been translated to him.

Thursday, Friday, and today we hid in the dog-woods to watch the soldiers. Elisabeth's eye was on Pierre, though he has not yet shown up wearing the coat she made him. Baron von Steuben, for all his arm-waving and swearing, is proving to be a good instructor and he's now learned enough English to curse directly at the men. His black coat comes to the top of his boots and flares out like a dress with his long strides.

Azor comes to the field, too, but often disappears after rabbits. I so want him to find us and play.

March 16, 1778, Monday

It has been a sunny week, no clouds, and the hills are greener each day. We can hear frogs at the creek and I am certain I saw a robin.

Yesterday we hung General Washington's shirts and such along our eastern fence to dry. I minded not so much the ironing and folding because the scent of fresh air has now filled our house.

Helen has taken up all Mama's mending and this morning baked a chocolate cake. She let Sally stir and lick.

Mrs. Washington sent Oney to ask our help. Tomorrow is a celebration for Saint Patrick's Day and she has many pies to bake. I'm glad she needs no eggs.

March 17, 1778, Tuesday

Sunny, breezy cool. We stood on the hill to watch the soldiers, our shawls wrapped tight. All afternoon there were blasts from muskets and cannons, mixed with rising puffs of smoke. The trill of fifes and steady rat-a-tat of drums made for a most festive mood. I hoped to see a drummer boy wearing the shirt I made.

After drills, the soldiers began a game called "Long Bullet," where they piled cannon balls in a heap, then stood back. With another ball they took turns seeing who could roll the longest and hardest and knock down the most.

We went in to help Mama with chores, then just before sundown returned to our hiding spot. There was the Commander in Chief George Washington playing catch with his officers! This turned into a game of wickets, using bent twigs poked into the ground for tiny gates. The ball they batted about was probably like the one we made Johnny out of deer hide.

I wondered if we were still at war, such was the sound of men's laughter and music. (This is Saint Patrick's Day, but who *is* Saint Patrick?)

March 18, 1778, Wednesday

When we woke again to drums and fifes I thought the soldiers were still celebrating. But on coming downstairs and hurrying through our breakfast, we realized the drumbeat was slower. I wanted not to go outside. If another woman was being drummed out of the army I would feel worse than if it were a man—I know not why, but I would.

Later Papa reported it had been an officer!—for perjury and other offenses.

March 20, 1778, Friday

Sunshine all yesterday and today. More buds on the trees, but not quite blossoms. We hiked to the creek—Elisabeth, Helen, Sally, and I—and found our secret pool. It is shallow with a sandy bottom, and as it's in the sun most of the day, it was not as icy as the running river.

Shrieking with cold we stripped down to our bare skin, jumped in heads under, then in an instant jumped out to dry ourselves with our skirts. We sat on the bank to let the sun dry our hair. Helen is smiling more. She knows not when her baby will be born, but the size of her belly seems to say "soon."

March 21, 1778, Saturday

Such a dark storm moved in this morning, so swiftly. Sally and I heard thunder while milking and quickly finished. We ran from the barn to the house in a blowing downpour, spilling much from our bucket. It rained hard all day. What we can see of the road from our window is a river of mud. In the distance was the sound of drums and fifes.

"Why are the men drilling even in the rain?" I asked Papa.

He said, "Von Steuben promised General Washington that he would turn our soldiers into an army and that is precisely what he is doing, Abby."

March 23, 1778, Monday

Still dark and rainy. We had to go to Headquarters as Monday is always Washday, rain or not. Such mud for our poor wagon. Helen came with me as Elisabeth is feverish and coughing.

Mrs. Washington and Mrs. Knox were in the kitchen — Mrs. Knox is so round I think she, too, is expecting a baby. They insisted we dry off before returning outside (to become soaked yet again!). I was sitting on a little stool by the kettle, my face and hands to the fire, when I felt something wet poke my side. I turned to see Azor, his nose now on my lap, and wagging his tail.

"Hullo, boy." I petted behind his ears and hugged his neck. When my hand felt the cloth on his back I could not believe mine eyes. Azor was wearing Elisabeth's coat!

The sleeves had been pulled up over his front paws and as it was a short waistcoat, it buttoned under his belly. Elisabeth's coat fit Azor!

It is late, the laundry is hanging through the house, still damp, and we girls are upstairs in our nightgowns. Elisabeth is shivering with fever — I have not the heart to tell her about Azor's new clothes.

March 24, 1778, Tuesday

As it is still raining, we are late returning the General's laundry. All morning we used hot irons with the hopes of drying things faster. It was almost suppertime before we drove to Headquarters. Papa covered the top of the wagon with planks of wood from the barn to keep the clothes dry underneath.

There in the parlour with Mr. Washington was von Steuben and Pierre and Alexander Hamilton, all speaking in a cheerful mixture of English and French. And there by the fire was Azor, having himself a nap, snug in his handsome blue coat.

What am I to tell Elisabeth?

March 27, 1778, Friday

Finally the storm broke. It has been sunny with just a few clouds in the afternoons bringing light rain, thus the roads are still muddy.

I was in the barn loft, playing dolls with Sally, when Papa came in the small door with a neighbour. When they began speaking in low voices I put my finger to Sally's lips, then mine, for they knew not we were directly above them.

"Why did you kill him?" Papa asked.

Sally and I looked at each other, wide-eyed, not daring to breathe.

"General Wayne told me to."

"A general told you to kill one of his men? Come now, this makes no sense."

"'Tis true. Every morning this same soldier has been coming into my barn and stealing a chicken. Every morning for a week, Edward. I reported it to General Wayne. He was sitting at a table writing a letter and would not look up at me. Finally I asked the General, I said, 'What shall I do?' General Wayne dipped his pen in the inkwell, kept writing, and without looking at me he said, 'Oh, just shoot him.'"

I could see through the crack in the floor that Papa's shoulders sagged and he was shaking his head. In a soft voice he said, "So thou shot the poor fellow?"

There were several moments of silence. "Yes," said the man. "He's buried by my south fence. No one knows but thee."

The rest of the day Papa was quiet. Sally and I spoke not about what we had heard.

March 28, 1778, Saturday

Baths after supper. (Papa always goes into the barn to brush Buttercup, so we shall have privacy.) We set the tub by the fire, but Helen is too broad to fit. She bent over to dip her head therein so I could wash her hair. She is very dear to us and this afternoon mentioned her dead husband for the first time.

"Today is my anniversary — we would have been married one year," was all she said.

Mama hung the lantern outside the door so Papa would know we were dressed and he could come dump out the bathwater. Before bed we popped corn and ate spice cake, sitting on the rug in front of the hearth. Color has returned to Elisabeth's cheeks, but she is still coughing. She sat in the rocker with Johnny, Mama's quilt tucked around them both.

"Abby," she said. "Hast thou seen Pierre? Is he wearing my coat, hast he mentioned my name?"

Helen glanced at me, because I had told her the story. How I wished I could spare Elisabeth shame and heartbreak, but too soon she would be well enough to visit Headquarters and one of these days Azor would be there, too. Maybe I should tell the truth.

I looked her in the eye and said, "I have seen Pierre, but he was not wearing thy coat."

April 1, 1778, Wednesday
Rain.

April 2, 1778, Thursday
Windy and cold.

April 3, 1778, Friday
Lucy came to visit! During tea she untied her bonnet, took it off, and handed it to me.

"Mama says I'm to return it, Abby."

We all were quiet. I was shocked by her appearance. Whoever had shaved her head had hacked away so that her hair was growing in uneven patches. She kept her eyes down. I tried to imagine what punishment her parents had threatened her with, that would have forced Lucy — willful, headstrong Lucy — to go out among people with a shaved head, no bonnet. I wanted to cry, she looked so drawn.

Mama gave one of her laced scarves to Lucy and showed her how to wrap it over her head. "Thou art pretty, dear," Mama told her.

Lucy said softly, "Thank you, Mrs. Stewart."

We crowded at the door to watch her walk away, up the road, and around the bend to her home.

April 4, 1778, Saturday

Mrs. Hewes brought news that a dancing master from New York is lodging at the DeWees house, down the hall from her room.

"He is small and limber," she told us, "yet old enough to be a grandfather. He plans to teach the officers and their wives how to dance."

When she said his name is Mr. John Trotter, I laughed so loud Mama and Papa stared at me. I know it was not polite, but his name makes me think of a dancing horse.

April 5, 1778, Sunday

A great commotion along the road met us on our way back from church.

Major General Charles Lee was finally freed by the Redcoats after more than a year in prison. I saw him on horseback as he rode up to Headquarters with drums and fifes escorting him. A grand dinner was given in his honour. Papa presented him with a new pair of shoes before the candles were lit, but when Papa came home, he was furious.

"He talks without listening, that man, and he has the foulest mouth I've ever heard use English. He was rude to Mrs. Washington, rude to the servants, and rude to me. Do ye think he was thankful that someone gave him new shoes when many men are still without?"

Papa slammed his fist on the table. "No. This is what he said, in front of the Commander in Chief and the other generals: 'I prefer pumps with a buckle. Must I wear garden slippers made for peasants?'"

April 6, 1778, Monday

Elisabeth and I learned something else about Major General Charles Lee and it wasn't nice.

When we arrived at Headquarters to pick up the wash, the long table was set for breakfast, but the officers and General Washington were only drinking tea, not eating.

Billy Lee whispered to us, "They's all waiting on Mr. Charles Lee to get out of bed."

We tiptoed upstairs to avoid the creaks. Just

past Mrs. Washington's closed door was another small bedroom and from behind its door we heard loud snoring. Elisabeth and I collected the laundry from the hallway, and hurried downstairs.

Oney was in the kitchen with Billy Lee and both were upset, whispering.

"Shame," she said, her hand on her hip. "That man don't deserve to be in the company of Mr. and Mrs. Wash'ton. He got stone drunk lass night and vomitted on the missus' finest tablecloth, then had to be carried to bed and now he's making everyone wait for breakfast. Shame, for shame. And yesterday bein' the Lord's Day."

Billy Lee shook his head. When we stepped down into the kitchen he handed us a small sack of kitchen cloths that needed to be washed, and he was still shaking his head when we left.

In the wagon we wrapped our shawls over our hair to keep the wind off. Elisabeth said, "Art thou going to tell Papa about General Lee?"

"No," said I. "It shall just give him a fit. He's likely to march over and take back his shoes and that might start another war."

April 7, 1778, Tuesday

Four other soldiers have been freed by the British and as they were being escorted to Headquarters we ran into the road, hoping one of them would be Mr. Fitzgerald, but no.

A young general arrived and is quartered with the Havard family. He has a fancy name — Marquis de Lafayette — and when he and Pierre speak to each other in French, they sound like two birds singing.

Mrs. Washington let Elisabeth and me serve tea to them. Lafayette has reddish hair, a narrow face, and a long pointed nose, which looks pinched on the end — he's not at all attractive, but he is quite cheerful. He holds his tea cup with his little finger in the air and laughs high and loud. I liked him, but Elisabeth said he needs to bathe.

"Also," she said, "the fellow should pick his teeth, for there's meat between them from last night's dinner."

This is the ninth day of high winds and cold.

April 9, 1778, Thursday

Johnny burned his little hand this morning and it's all my fault. I'm just sick, he cries so.

I was lifting the kettle lid, to pour in more oats, but from outside there came a loud boom of cannons. I was so startled I dropped the lid. Though heavy, it rolled like a shilling toward the rug where Johnny was and tipped over onto his hand. Poor Johnny! His eyes went wide then he began to howl.

I am upset at myself, but mostly cross — again — at the Army. I wish they would leave! Cannons are the worst — they're loud and wind carries the noise to our front step.

Mrs. Hewes brought ointment. Johnny lay in her arms staring up at her face while she rocked him. Finally he slept.

She said that she and Mr. Trotter are becoming acquainted. He plays the fiddle and has tried to teach her a minuet.

"I know not why the man thought he could start a dancing school at Valley Forge," she said after laying Johnny in his cradle. "The officers are busy and their wives are knitting night and day. Thank goodness the ladies think socks for the soldiers are more important than learning a jig."

April 10, 1778, Friday

Loud knocking on our door after all were in bed. Voices downstairs. A candle was lit. I could see it through the floor cracks, but I was so sleepy I pulled the quilt over my head. Soon there was the sound of boots coming upstairs.

"Abigail, Elisabeth." It was Papa. "Mr. Smith is here. Have ye seen Lucy?"

No, I shook my head. Helen stirred on her cot. Elisabeth buried her shoulders under the quilt with Sally. We were embarrassed to have Mr. Smith see us in our nightgowns.

"Do ye know where she is?" he asked.

"No, sir."

Mr. Smith held his lantern high, filling our room with light. He looked under our beds and in the wardrobe. Shadows on his face made him look sad.

"Forgive me, Edward, for waking thee," he said. "Lucy stepped out before supper to bring an egg from the barn. She never returned. We thought she might be with thy daughters. Lord in Heaven, what will I tell her mother?" He turned for the hall, his light sweeping across our beds and chimney, then down the shadowy stairs.

When we were alone again we began whispering.

"Where has Lucy gone?"

"Did she run off with a soldier?"

"Poor Lucy."

It was Helen who took our hands in the dark and said, "Let's pray for Lucy. Let's pray she shant harm herself."

April 12, 1778, Sunday

Lucy's family was in church, but they sat in back. I avoided looking at Mrs. Smith, but outside by the corral she caught my arm. Her eyes were wet and full of sorrow. The wind blew our skirts against our legs.

"Abby," she said, "if thou dost see Lucy, tell her to come home, please. All is forgiven, tell her."

"Yes, ma'am."

April 13, 1778, Monday

Washday, again bleached shirts and such. It takes all of us all day, from sunrise to supper — Mama, Sisters, Helen, and I — to wash, bleach, starch, rinse, wring out, hang up, iron, and fold. Papa keeps the fire hot and he has built a tiny pen by the hearth for Johnny so he shant crawl into the coals.

It was too windy to hang bed sheets on the fence. I shall be pleased when the Army leaves so our chores won't be so many.

April 14, 1778, Tuesday

After delivering the laundry to Headquarters, we took the long way home. As we came to Joseph Mann's cabin we saw several horses out front and one of the generals pulling himself up into his saddle. He commands the troops from North Carolina and Georgia, and is quartered here. He gave a friendly salute to Joseph, who was carrying firewood inside. Though Joseph is a freed Negro and a good honest man, two of the officers spit at his feet before galloping away. I was so provoked I wanted to throw a stone at the men, but the wagon seat was too high off the ground to reach one.

We crossed Valley Creek and soon came to Slab Tavern. Mrs. Washington had a note for us to give the innkeeper.

The tavern was crowded but we noticed Pierre.

He was sitting at a large side table and unlike the other men and officers with him, he smiled at us. Elisabeth and I curtsied. Pierre stood, then began making his way among the tables toward us.

"Dear ladies," he said, bowing slightly. He took Elisabeth's hand, kissed the ends of her fingers, then did the same with mine. We both were lost for words, but I knew from the color rising in Elisabeth's cheeks that she was well-pleased with his manners.

We were interrupted by the innkeeper, a gruff man, who took Mrs. Washington's note, broke the wax seal, read the message, then crumpled it in his large hand.

"Tell Her Highness that I have no plates to spare, nor cups, nor soap, nor whatever she might think of next." He pulled open the door and pointed us out.

That's when we saw Baron von Steuben coming up the path with Azor.

April 15, 1778, Wednesday
About yesterday:

At first Elisabeth did not realize Azor was wearing her blue coat, because he now also had a red

107

sash draped over his back like a little soldier. We walked quickly past and not until we were in the wagon did she turn to study him. With her mouth open she looked at me with astonishment, pointed to Azor, and said, "Abby?"

That's all she said for the rest of the day.

Everyone is in bed now, except Mama is downstairs rocking Johnny. While we were fastening our nightcaps, Elisabeth stood with me at the window for a few minutes, looking out at the stars. Finally she whispered, "Please do not tell Mama who's wearing my coat, dost thou promise, Abby?"

I promised.

April 16, 1778, Thursday

The wind continues.

I woke in the night to the scratching of branches against the house. Sally woke up crying. She said she saw a man climb up the trellis by our window and he was waving his arm back and forth. I looked out, then tucked her in again.

"It's just our big old apple tree, Sally. Go back to sleep."

April 17, 1778, Friday

Mrs. Hewes invited us for afternoon tea. The wind was rough and as it was nearly an hour's walk, we dressed in wool and Mama carried Johnny inside her cloak.

Colonel DeWees has a fine stone house with many chimneys. The basement has become quarters for the army baker, a German named Christopher Ludwig. He uses several ovens to turn out all the bread needed, about sixty loaves an hour.

We sat in a parlour by a blazing hearth. The next room also had a fireplace and a broad plank floor where there was the sound of feet tapping.

"That's Mr. Trotter," she explained, "practicing. Sugar?" She cut off the end of the sugar cone and dropped it in Mama's cup, then one in mine, and all around, even Sally's.

"He has no students yet," she continued, "but last Wednesday evening that room saw a splendid theatrical performance."

"Dost thou mean a play?" I asked.

"Why, yes, dear. General Washington himself was in attendance, including several officers. There are plans for a production next month of the drama *Cato*. I hadn't realized how the General loves theater — he's quite a devotee."

Our visit was shortened because Johnny began to fuss and would not quiet down.

April 20, 1778, Monday

It is nine o'clock at night with a furious wind blowing. It is most frightening to look outside because the sky is red from fires burning on Mount Joy. Papa says mayhaps a spark from someone's chimney was carried by the wind. It has been six hours and still we see a glow from our window. I have just blown out my candle and my pen can see its way across the paper . . .

April 21, 1778, Tuesday

A messenger came this morning with a letter for me. I was alone in the house with Johnny because Papa had taken everyone in the wagon to look at Mount Joy.

The letter was from Lucy, telling me where she was.

After reading it I threw it into the fire.

"Tell not a soul," were the words below her signature.

And so I cannot even write about it.

April 26, 1778, Sunday

We woke this morning to silence. The wind has stopped! It blew hard for twenty-four days straight and we lost many branches in the orchards. The sun this morning feels warm like Spring. We girls ran out to feel grass under our feet.

The dogwoods are in bloom. Such beauty. Their branches look like they're wearing thick cotton leggings.

The fires on Mount Joy burned themselves out. Only steam rises from the hillsides.

April 29, 1778, Wednesday

Mama and I visited Mrs. Hewes to invite her to a wedding tomorrow. While water boiled for tea she led us through the various public rooms, showing us paintings on the walls, lovely scenics and portraits.

On entering the taproom we heard loud voices arguing at a corner table. Wanting not to interrupt, we quickly went through another door to the library, but we did hear this much: Colonel DeWees was complaining to three generals that soldiers had once again raided one of his buildings.

"Lumber and stones are missing!" he thundered. "How shalt I ever reconstruct the previous damage if the Army keeps stealing from the very people it's supposed to protect?"

We returned to the main hearth and over tea wondered in whispers how much longer we must bear with these soldiers.

Papa has stopped telling Mama how many tools and eggs have disappeared from our own barn. I'm thankful Brownie has not been stolen, else we shant have butter or cream.

April 30, 1778, Thursday

The wedding was held in perfect sunshine on the wide lawn in front of Headquarters. The bride is our friend Ann Pritchard from Chester County, and Papa has made her family's shoes for fifteen years. Her dress was white linen with lace along the sleeves and hem.

There were many tears among the older women watching, and some of the younger ones. Helen cried because the wedding reminded her she is a wife no more, but why Elisabeth wept I know not. Mayhaps because her Bounty Coat is being worn by a dog.

The groom we had not met before today. He is a cavalryman from Virginia. How handsome he looked in uniform. His tall riding boots were polished to match his scabbard. When the chaplain pronounced them man and wife, the groom threw his tricorn in the air and swept Ann into his arms. There were cheers and huzzahs as he lifted her into a carriage.

They are staying now at the Potters' in the small upstairs room above the kitchen.

After the wedding, Mrs. Smith came over to us. One glance at her sad eyes and I had to look away. Oh, I wish to God Lucy had not begged me to keep silent.

May 1, 1778, Friday

We were awakened at dawn by drumming and fifes. It was a jaunty tune. We hurried out to see soldiers parading and singing at the tops of their voices.

"What is it, Papa?" we asked.

He laughed. "Of course, how couldst I have forgotten? It's May Day."

Such celebrations all day. The soldiers had put up May Poles last night in each brigade, with streamers hanging down. They marched and sang in formation, their tricorns adorned with white blossoms from the dogwoods.

We watched from the hill while men played wickets and catch and Long Bullet. We could smell meat roasting from a huge pit barbeque by Headquarters, on the Schuylkill's south bank.

Papa took off his hat and waved it at the soldiers. "By God," he said to us, "it's about time those good men enjoy themselves."

May 2, 1778, Saturday

We have thrown open the doors front and back, and the small window in the kitchen. How good the warm spring air smells. All day we cleaned: scrubbed soot off the walls, raked the coals, Sally and I swept the floor with wet sand to gather up all the dust. Elisabeth and Mama moved beds and cupboards and wardrobes to mop. Helen carried the feather quilts out to hang over what is left of our fence—about fifty feet along the lane in front of our house is all!

General Washington made a new rule. Drummers and fifers may practice just twice a day, not whenever they please. From four to five o'clock in the afternoon and from five to six o'clock in the morning.

Mama is furious.

The noise wakes up Johnny and she does not want him fussing that early. He is now five months old and crawling everywhere. He crawled up six steps but knew not how to crawl down. He turned to look for us and when he did he lost his balance, tumbled headfirst, and raised such a wail we could not console him.

He has a bump above his right eye that is purple, but do you think he learned his lesson? No. He crawls for the stairs and one of us must watch him at all times. We are sore relieved when he finally goes to sleep at night.

This is why Mama is mad about drums and whistles—she calls them—playing at five o'clock in the morning.

May 3, 1778, Sunday

A clatter of many horses and two coaches interrupted our evening prayers. Papa got up from the table to look out.

Lights were blazing at Headquarters and there was the faint sound of singing.

"It seems someone has brought the General good news," Papa said to us when he returned from the window.

May 4, 1778, Monday

This morning while getting the laundry we heard much excited talk in the kitchen and front room of Headquarters.

Mrs. Washington wore an apron over her cotton dress and was overseeing the baking of pies and gingerbread. A roast pig turned on the spit, its juice filling the drip pan. General Greene's wife and several other ladies were helping. Their skirts filled the room with color and rustling.

I glanced in the other room. General Washington stood by the hearth, his arm on the mantel. He was smiling and listening to his officers.

"What hast happened?" I whispered to Billy Lee.

"Oh, Miss, the best news ever," he said. He nodded toward Pierre and Lafayette, who were surrounded by officers clapping them on their backs and shaking their hands.

Mrs. Washington leaned over to smile at us. Her sleeves were pushed up to her elbows and there was flour on her chin. "It's an alliance with France, Abby. They are coming to help us fight the British, praise God. We might be back in our own beds sooner than we think."

That explained why Pierre and Lafayette were having affection lavished on them. They were no longer just aides-de-camp, they were now our allies.

As Elisabeth and I carried the sacks down the hallway, we saw Mrs. Greene move gracefully into the parlour, also to shake Pierre's hand, then Lafayette's. She spoke perfect French! By the time we were going out the door, which stood open for the breeze, she was in a cheerful conversation with the two Frenchmen, Alexander Hamilton, and another aide named John Laurens.

How I wish I could speak that pretty language, too.

May 5, 1778, Tuesday

Ten straight days of sunshine!

Helen is so large with child she has trouble lying down at nights. Papa brought her cot down by the fire and raised the back so she can sleep sitting up. She complains not, but I know she is glad she doesn't have to climb the stairs.

Lucy's parents are sick with worry. They have come over twice this week. What am I to do? If I tell, Lucy shall feel betrayed, but if I keep her secret . . .

Is it proper to let her family suffer so?

May 6, 1778, Wednesday

What a grand day! It is late now, and I will try to put it all down before my candle goes.

At dawn we woke to the call of a fife and a single drummer. Such a beautiful morning, cool with sunshine, birds have returned to the trees, making nests and song. Finally there are flowers! The slopes of Mount Joy and Mount Misery are purple and red with azaleas; even the shade is bright with yellow from blooming laurel.

From 9:00 until 10:30 a hush fell over the valley. Everywhere soldiers with their officers knelt together in their brigades. Papa rode the outskirts of camp and said the chaplains were leading the men in prayer and thanksgiving; everyone is so humbly grateful for the French Alliance. We could hear voices rise with the singing of hymns, like an echo rolling across the valley. It was a most joyful sound and though I could hear no words, it filled me with peace.

When the singing stopped we climbed the hill to look down toward Varnum's quarters. There in perfectly straight rows the soldiers stood at attention. General Washington was on his gray horse, most dignified, flanked by his generals, all in sharp uniform. Papa explained this was "inspection."

We watched Baron von Steuben give orders. Each brigade responded in perfect form: turning, marching, and kneeling to load their muskets. (Azor, wearing his coat and sash, appeared nervous from the horses and guns; he ran off into the brush.)

Neighbours gathered to watch and there were excited cries of children when 13 cannons — six pounders — were rolled up to the rear of Conway's Brigade. General Washington gave a signal with a smooth wave of his hat and from the hill cannons began firing, one after another, a "13-gun salute."

It was so loud Johnny screwed up his face and would not stop crying. Sally held her hands over her ears. Papa raised his arm and cheered. I found myself with tears. I know not why, but there was beauty about the soldiers lined up so proud and clean, the cannons firing for joy, not war.

When the last echo from the last boom faded away, there began what Papa called a *feu de joie*. Now, one by one, muskets began to fire along the front rank from right to left, then down the second rank from left to right. The shots rippled back and forth, raising smoke like dozens of chimneys. The whole effect filled every one of us with excitement and hope — this was our army! No longer weak or frightened or cold. This *feu de joie* truly was a "fire of joy."

When the soldiers and officers — hundreds and hundreds of them — burst into cheer shouting "Huzzah! Long live the King of France!" Mama covered her face with her apron and wept with happiness.

My candle! Too short . . .

May 7, 1778, Thursday

To finish about yesterday:

When the ranks of muskets had quieted, there began another 13-gun salute from the hill, followed by another *feu de joie*, then the men again cheered. This time they shouted, "Long live the friendly European powers!"

Then once more the 13 cannons blasted, one after another, and once more the musket shots rippled through the ranks. Such smoke rose and filled the valley. By now every neighbour, child, and soldier was cheering and we heard the words, "Long live the American states!"

Johnny finally stopped crying, but he had hiccups and an unhappy face. Helen carried him into the house so he could settle down.

Papa stood behind Mama with his arms around her as we watched the soldiers file out. General Washington rode toward Headquarters on his beautiful horse, his arm waving his tricorn. We could not see his face, but we did hear him shout "Huzzah!" again and again.

Papa said, "Darling, if ever our Army was ready to stand up to the British, I believe it is now." We have just finished supper. The days are getting longer so I am writing by the last bits of sunlight.

I can see Headquarters. Our door downstairs is open for the cool night air, and we can hear laughter and singing. All afternoon officers and their ladies rode up to attend Washington's celebration. I wonder if Mrs. Washington baked enough pies!

Papa said that being allied with the French might help us shoo the Redcoats out of America for good.

May 8, 1778, Friday

Helen has been uncomfortable all day and unable to eat. Mama said this means her baby is ready to be born.

Now it is late, nearly half-past ten o'clock. Papa and Sally are sleeping, but Mama is downstairs with Helen. Every few minutes she cries out, then apologizes for crying.

"It's all right, Helen, dear," Mama tells her. "Thou mayest cry as loud as y'want."

May 9, 1778, Saturday

Before breakfast Papa left with the wagon to get Mrs. Hewes. Poor Helen. She is exhausted.

2 P.M.—Johnny and Sally are both having naps on the rug. There is sunshine on them from the side window. How they sleep through all our voices is a mystery.

Mrs. Hewes soothes Helen with a wet cloth. Now she and Mama are making Helen get up and walk around. She is so tired she cries without tears. "Thou must not die," I whisper to myself.

5 P.M.—Papa took Sally and Johnny to the Potters' where they shall stay the night.

May 10, 1778, Sunday

Am nearly too tired to write this, but Mama says there must be a record. It is four o'clock in the morning. The sun is not yet up.

A baby girl was born 15 minutes ago.

May 11, 1778, Monday

We have all had some rest and so it is easier for me to write.

Helen is sleeping in Mama's bed, her tiny daughter at her side. She has named her Olivia and she is a beautiful pink with a crown of red hair. Now I remember her father, the poor soldier in the hut whose feet were cut off. He had red hair, too, and the most gentle blue eyes. I sorrow that he is not alive to see his family.

Mrs. Potter came by with a pot of stew and corn-cakes. Mrs. Adams brought three apple pies. I knew not what to say when we opened the door and saw Mrs. Fitzgerald standing there with a basket on her arm.

"For the new baby," she said. She turned and walked quickly down the road. We lifted the cloth. There inside was a small quilt, booties, and a rag doll with a pretty blue dress.

May 12, 1778, Tuesday

We are a day late doing the General's laundry, but Mama said sometimes that is the way of things. We have strung two lines outside between the trees and fence, to let the sun do its quick work. It is much more pleasant to iron and fold when shirts and such dry in the fresh air instead of a sooty house.

Mama is teaching Helen how to nurse her baby and keep her clean and warm. I held Olivia and rocked her. Oh, she's beautiful.

May 13, 1778, Wednesday

We heard today that a girl with shorn hair was seen at one of the hospitals, working as a nurse. Mr. Smith and Papa left immediately to find her, and everyone is praying that it is Lucy.

All day I worried if I should tell where Lucy really is and worried myself so much that I got a terrible stomachache.

Reverend Currie came for supper, but I stayed in my bed listening through the floor cracks. He said a drummer boy was given 50 lashes for trading shirts with a British soldier. How this was discovered, he didn't say. Also, a soldier was given 200 lashes after he was caught running away from his commanding officer.

Reverend Currie asked our prayers for the great number of soldiers who are sick. Many are dying of the Pox and other infections. They are being buried naked so that their clothes can be passed on to others in need.

May 14, 1778, Thursday

The girl with shorn hair was not Lucy, which I knew it wouldn't be. At breakfast we prayed for her and for the soldiers. I silently asked God to show me what to do.

There are Indians in camp! Oneidas and Tuscaroras. I saw them walk along the road toward Headquarters, dressed in a curious assortment of deerskin leggings and soldier coats, feather ornaments and tricorns. They have volunteered to help General Washington.

"I want to see the Indians," Sally demanded. "Up close, please!"

I was fearful, but Papa said not to be. "There are Mohegan and Stockbridge Indians already serving the brigades from Massachusetts and Connecticut, Abby. And they are as loyal as any of the other men."

Still, I stayed home. Two hours later Sally burst in the front door.

"Abby, I saw one. He had tattoos on his arms and face and guess what he did!"

"What."

"He walked into Mrs. Washington's kitchen. There was a hot roast beef on the table and he grabbed a chunk of it with his finger and thumb and he twisted it out and he walked to the front door right past me — right past me — and he began to eat and dripped grease all over the floor. Abby, I saw an Indian and I feared not."

Sally is now in Mama's room telling her adventure to Helen and Elisabeth.

When I see how tenderly Helen holds her new little daughter, I wonder if I must now go to Mrs. Smith. How she must ache for Lucy.

May 17, 1778, Sunday

Baby Olivia is now seven days old and it is so warm and pleasant out Helen brought her to church.

Mrs. Hewes told us afterward that there was another theatrical production at the Bakehouse last Monday and the audience was most lively. The play was *Cato*. I wish I could go see the next one, but no children are allowed.

May 18, 1778, Monday

Washday.

We put Olivia in the cradle and Johnny in the pen, which makes him mad. He hollers and bangs his spoon against the wood.

I carried him outside so he could crawl in the grass while we hung the wash. I turned my back on him for just a moment and when I looked there he was in the middle of the road and horses were coming.

"Johnny, thou art too little to play here," I scolded as I lifted him to my hip. His mouth turned down and he let out such a wail Papa came over. Papa clapped his hands and set Johnny on his shoulders for a "Bumpity Ride." Soon he started laughing and I was able to finish with the clothesline.

At sunset I hurried down the lane to the Smith cottage. I had made up my mind. In a quick breath I told them Lucy is safe, that she shall return when her hair has grown to her shoulders.

Mrs. Smith wept with relief and her husband wiped his own cheek.

"Thank you, Abigail," he said.

After supper I wrote a letter to Lucy, saying I could no longer bear to see her parents' sorrow.

"But they know not where you stay," I wrote, "and for now I shant tell a soul."

May 19, 1778, Tuesday

General Lafayette and some of our troops are marching toward Germantown. They crossed the Schuylkill at Swede's Ford last night about midnight. Papa said 100 Indians came, too, and they are all camped at Barren Hill, twelve miles from Philadelphia. He said there may or may not be a battle.

General Washington says from now on the soldiers are free on Fridays, they don't have to drill. This is because the streams are warm enough to wash clothes and to bathe — but they may stay in the water no longer than ten minutes so they do not get a chill.

Oney came to say Mrs. Washington would enjoy the company of one of us to visit some hospitals at the southern edge of camp. Elisabeth refuses to go anymore, Helen has a baby to care for, and the three Potter girls have not been vaccinated for the Pox (we were last year).

Now that I'm ready to go to bed and am

remembering the last time I visited sick soldiers with Mrs. Washington, I'm sorry I said yes.

May 20, 1778, Wednesday

A lieutenant drove us in the wagon, south along Gulph Road to the Quaker meeting house. There were cots from one end of the room to the other.

The stench was worse than a latrine and there was a sharp odor I could not recognize. To keep from gagging I covered my mouth and nose with my shawl. Why the windows and doors were not open to let in fresh air I know not. I followed Mrs. Washington as she worked her way down the crowded rows, talking to the soldiers who were awake and praying with them. She drew not away from smells or the sight of amputated feet.

In a corner of the room a doctor was giving inoculations for the Pox. One soldier whose cheeks were covered with sores tossed on his bed in a fever, moaning and crying out. He was shivering even with a blanket over him. The doctor took a feather and with the sharp end of the quill, scooped it into one of the man's oozing pox. Then he turned to a waiting soldier who had his sleeve rolled up and a fresh cut on his arm from the doctor's pen knife (I was sickened, watching).

Into this fresh cut the doctor dabbed a bit of the goo and said, "There you go, friend. Thou shalt soon have a fever, but worry not. More die from the disease than vaccinations."

This was repeated with nine soldiers who'd been waiting outside in the sunshine.

When we climbed up to the wagon seat we saw a graveyard across the lane. Two men were finishing digging a grave. Beside them lay the thin shape of a body rolled into a blanket. Without a word the men lifted, then dropped the body — naked — into the grave, each holding an edge of the blanket. While one shoveled dirt, the other carried the blanket to the hospital and handed it through the door.

Our wagon dipped down into a gully and as it rose again over a hill I turned around. I could see through a window that the blanket was being spread over one of the sick men. I glanced back at the cemetery.

"Why are there no names on the graves?" I asked Mrs. Washington.

She smiled. Sunlight was on her face and she closed her eyes to enjoy the warmth. "My dear, it is one of those puzzles. Quakers, God bless them, are against war. They do not honour soldiers, so that is why their graves are marked not."

May 21, 1778, Thursday

Elisabeth and I were with Papa at the north end of our orchards, trimming branches that had broken in the winds last month. A coach passed us, its horses at a high trot with a coachman riding above the rear wheel. Sally was already running from the house (barefoot still, as Papa has had no time to make her shoes).

Papa laughed and said, "Go on, girls," and we, too, ran with Sally.

When we saw the very plump lady stepping down from the coach with a tiny infant in her arms, we cried "Hello, Mrs. Knox!" She waved and called us over to look at her new baby.

A handsome soldier inside the coach helped her down then stepped out with a cane. He wore high-heeled boots and was limping quite a bit. He took Mrs. Knox's elbow to guide her into Headquarters.

"Girls," she said to us, "this is Mr. Benedict

Arnold, my official escort. Would you like to take turns holding the baby when we get inside?"

Sally went first, sitting on the stool by the kitchen hearth. Mrs. Washington cooed and fussed over the tiny thing, and not until we were home did I realize no one said if it was a boy or a girl or what its name was.

While Elisabeth held the baby, we could hear Benedict Arnold in the parlour talking to General Washington. He was describing his horrible wound from the Saratoga Campaign seven months ago and how he is only now able to hobble about with great pain.

While I held the baby — only for a quick moment — Mrs. Washington told us there will be no more plays at the Bakehouse.

"Can ye imagine?" she said. "Of all the things Congress has to worry about and they pass a silly resolution. This is what it says." She pulled a piece of parchment from her apron pocket, unfolded it, and held it at arm's length to read: "'Any person holding an office under the United States, who shall attend a theatrical performance shall be dismissed from service.'" Mrs. Washington handed the page to Mrs. Knox so she could read for herself then said, "Sometimes government has the most ridiculous notions."

May 25, 1778, Monday

When Elisabeth and I arrived at Headquarters to pick up the laundry, there were several ladies dressed in their best, saying farewell to one another.

Billy Lee told us, "There's soon to be a battle, so the wives are going home."

"Battle?"

"Oh, not here, Miss. General Wash'ton will take his soldiers somewheres else to fight the Redcoats, don't you worry none. Not here, nosir."

May 26, 1778, Tuesday

Elisabeth and I were putting clean linen on our beds when Sally stomped upstairs, excited and out of breath.

"A soldier is here asking for thee, Beth. Hurry."

I looked at my older sister and could see her eyes brighten. "Is it Pierre?" she whispered.

"He said naught." Sally was already hurrying

downstairs, making a lot of noise for someone with bare feet.

Elisabeth smoothed her skirt. She smiled tenderly at me before turning for the stairs.

The soldier standing by the hearth looked proud in his uniform, white stirrups over new shoes, a tricorn under his arm, a handsome coat. When he smiled at her and I saw his top teeth were missing, I knew the handsome coat was the one made by Elisabeth.

I could not see her face.

"Yes?" she said softly.

We all dared not breathe. Helen was in the rocker with Johnny on her lap, Mama at the fire, Papa was sewing a piece of leather.

Sally stared at the soldier, then said, "Canst thou do this?" She stuck her tongue out through the space where her two new teeth were barely showing. "Look." But she spit by mistake and we all in one voice said, "Sally!"

The soldier laughed and reached over to pat her head. "I jess come by t' thank Miss Elisabeth Ann for making me a coat. No one ever done such a nice thing for me ever. Thank you, Miss. I'll be going now."

He shook Papa's hand, smiled again at Elisabeth, then stepped outside.

"Mister!" called Sally. "What is thy name?"

"Ben," he said. "Ben Valentine, Second Pennsylvania Brigade."

May 27, 1778, Wednesday

The soldiers who camped with General Lafayette outside Philadelphia a few days ago returned this morning in a drizzle. No shots were fired. Papa said it was just a drill.

It rained all day and was cold enough to wear our wool stockings.

Elisabeth was gloomy. "I wish I had been kinder to Ben Valentine," she told me in the barn while we milked Brownie.

"Thou wast not mean to him, Beth."

"No, but I could have offered him tea. He was good to come by, was he not, Abby?"

Odd, but I am no longer jealous of Elisabeth. She is much prettier than I, but she is not perfect. Today, I think she is even a bit heartsore.

May 28, 1778, Thursday

Rain and wind.

May 31, 1778, Sunday

It has been dark and rainy for five days. We all have colds so we stayed in. Papa led us in prayers and hymns instead of taking us to church. We can see that the soldiers are also inside. The valley is quiet with chimney smoke coming from the huts.

Johnny kept us amused by a new trick he's learned. He pops his lips. Also, he now can climb to the top of the stairs. He stays on his stomach and tries to crawl down backwards, but twice he bumped his chin and cried so loud, we carried him back to the rug. Papa made a gate at the bottom of the stairs from one of the cupboard doors so now Johnny must find something else to do.

Sally keeps asking me to tell more about Lucy.

"Do not worry, Sally. I promise she's safe."

June 1, 1778, Monday

The roads are muddy again, but now the sun has returned, warmer than before.

The soldiers practice until sundown so we are hearing cannons and muskets fired all day. Papa said General Washington is getting ready to move the Army to battle, but nearly 4,000 will stay behind — those who are sick or crippled.

Because the air is warm, there is a terrible stench as we ride at the edge of camp. Dead horses need to be buried — Papa said 1,500 have died! At night we hear crows and owls fly from their nests in the dark hillsides to pick at their carcasses and other butchered animals.

Washday.

June 2, 1778, Tuesday

We took Johnny to the creek after delivering the laundry to Headquarters. I held him while he kicked his chubby legs in the water and shrieked. He is six months old and will stand up and take a step if someone holds his arms. In his mouth, on his bottom gum, is a tiny white bulge where a tooth is trying to grow.

I like to hug him and twirl him over the stream so his feet skim the water. When he laughs I am so thankful he's alive — our first brother to make it through the winter.

I find myself more patient with Sally because my worry for Johnny has passed.

June 3, 1778, Wednesday

Reverend Currie delivered a letter for Mama. She sat at the table where there's light from our window, and carefully broke the seal. Her eyes fell to the signature.

"It's from Philadelphia, from your Auntie Hannie," she said. I watched Mama's face as she read silently. Finally she looked up.

"Girls, ye have a new cousin. His name is Matthew Robert and all is well. Bless Hannie, she's now got six little ones, my goodness. But here is the best part, listen:

'The baby is ever so tiny and needs constant attention as do the five others. I thank God your friend Lucy is here to help, for I know not how I would rest otherwise . . .'"

All heads turned to me as Mama continued to read.

"'. . . Lucy has asked me to relay her where-abouts to you. She is terribly quiet and I worry about her cough and lack of appetite. She was several days without food or shelter while making her way here, hiding in the forest from soldiers. Lucy begged to stay with us, until her hair has grown, for she is too full of shame to face her parents otherwise. I pray, for her mother's sake, that her hair grows quickly. Your loving sister, Hannie.'

"Why did she go all the way to Philadelphia?" Mama asked me.

I took a deep breath. "Lucy knew Hannie would not turn her away for they became fast friends when we visited in January. She knew she would be safe." Here I burst into tears, finally free of Lucy's secret.

Mama put her arms around me. "It's all right, dear."

June 4, 1778, Thursday

I was so happy yesterday but I'm not happy today.

We saw with our own eyes a soldier being hanged. We happened along the road just as the horse bolted from under the tree and the poor man kicked and struggled. His hands were tied behind his back, but he managed to free one hand and try to grab the noose. I burst into sobs, Elisabeth did, too. Oh, it was horrible, horrible — the poor man.

Talk on the road was that he was a spy and that one of his friends shall be hanged tomorrow. I hate the Army — I want them to leave!

June 7, 1778, Sunday

Beautiful drive to church. Daisies, white and yellow, are in bloom along the road and up the hillsides. We are a large family now with Helen and baby Olivia, Mama and Papa, Elisabeth, Sally and I, and our wiggly Johnny.

An announcement from the pulpit made us all break into cheers (something I have not before heard in church): The British have released six patriots from the Walnut Street jail in Philadelphia, they are in reasonably fair health, and they shall return to Valley Forge tomorrow. The name that made me want to cry for joy was this one:

Mr. William Fitzgerald.

June 8, 1778, Monday

Mrs. Fitzgerald was standing in the road looking south when we passed her on our way to pick up the wash from Headquarters. With her were her three littlest boys, standing straight, their faces clean and hair combed. They were about five, six, and seven years old, and the sight of them made my heart squeeze tight.

How brave she was to stand there, ready to meet her husband, to give him the tragic news about their five older sons. She seemed a different woman now that she knew she must be brave.

When Buttercup pulled the wagon around the bend and out of her sight, I broke down weeping, heavy sobs that would not stop. I was heartsore for Mrs. Fitzgerald, but thrilled her husband was safe. I felt sad for also hating Tom and that he'd not had a chance to grow up and be the good man his father is. I am very blue . . .

June 9, 1778, Tuesday

I am even more heartsore than yesterday.

Mrs. Washington left a few hours ago.

She is traveling back to Mount Vernon and I shall probably never see her again.

Elisabeth and I returned the wash about half-past nine this morning. Oney and Billy Lee were packing trunks and the other servants were up and down the stairs with things. The kitchen smelled of fresh apple pie and coffee, and several officers — I remember not their names — were talking with General Washington in the front room.

Billy Lee said to us, "Lady Wash'ton will be down soon, after her devotions, Misses. Then yous can say good-bye."

But I wanted not to say good-bye. So much kindness had come from her kitchen and her words. The long, cold winter had not seemed so lonesome because of her.

"Dear girls." We turned to see her coming down the stairs. She wore a dress of blue muslin with tiny white buttons up each sleeve. She seemed beautiful to me, though I remember how plain I'd thought she was at first.

We've known her just four months and I can say she is the most cheerful, loving person I have ever met. Never did I hear her say a cruel word or complain about her surroundings. Mama said at Mount Vernon Mrs. Washington has more than 300 slaves and a luxurious mansion. We are not of her social class and we had little to offer her, yet still she welcomed us as friends.

She gave us a small basket as we curtsied out the

door. "Inside there ye shall find a little something for your mother and yourselves, too. God bless ye, dear girls."

We hurried home. Mama put the basket on the table, and removed the cloth. Inside was a small leather pouch that jingled with coins. She peeked inside and read the attached note: "'40 shillings per month for Headquarters' laundry in addition to 4 shillings per dozen pieces for Mrs. Washington.'

"Why there must be a fortune here, my goodness. And what's this?" Mama lifted out a small stack of handkerchiefs, tied with a red satin ribbon. They were cotton trimmed with lace, folded neatly. There were ten, two for each of us and with them this note: "With fond wishes to Mrs. Stewart, Elisabeth, Abigail, Sally, and Helen Kern. We spent just a brief time together, but I shall always remember ye. Martha Washington."

June 10, 1778, Wednesday

The days are warm and drowsy.

We made soap with beet juice so it would turn pink, then we scented it with lavender. Helen and Sally gathered the flowers from along the creek then crushed the petals into a sweet-smelling oil. After mixing, we poured it into our wooden mould that we'd lined with a damp cloth. It must set 24 hours.

June 11, 1778, Thursday

By noon the soap was dry so we cut it into cakes with a wire. This is the most pleasant chore of them all. We boiled more lard and this time added carrot juice to make it yellowish, and crushed rosemary leaves for perfume.

Tomorrow Sally wants to use spinach for green, then add rose petals for scent. My opinion of green soap is this: It looks like something from the bottom of our well, but I wanted not to hurt Sally's feelings so kept this to myself. (My favourite is pink with a rosemary fragrance.) What a luxury to again have soap. I shall appreciate my bath even more, knowing our soldiers shant see their own homes for weeks to come.

June 12, 1778, Friday

Mama says the best thing about the Army leaving soon is that there shall be no more drums and whistles at five o'clock in the morning.

I shall be glad to see no more hangings.

Cannons and muskets still fire throughout the day.

Papa made a new butter churn. It hangs in the kitchen from a rafter by the front door. Every time one of us walks by we push it to swing. Sally finds this most amusing and because she is bossy, she has assigned us each a task:

I set aside the cream from Brownie's milk; Helen pours it in the top of the churn; Elisabeth corks it; then Sally gets to swing the barrel first. She pushed it so hard though, it banged into the wall. Papa has now re-hung it further into the room and raised it several inches so we won't bump our heads. He gave Sally a stick so she can reach it.

June 13, 1778, Saturday

We bathed today at the stream. Johnny thinks he can swim. He crawls fast from the bank, across the narrow sandy beach, then into the water. He cries not when his head goes under or when the current tries to carry him away. We must watch him every moment.

Next week we will leave him home with Mama so we can swim without worrying about him.

June 15, 1778, Monday

Our wash dries fast in the sun and breeze. The grass is wonderful under our bare feet.

Sally stepped on a wasp and it kept stinging her and even crawled up her ankle to sting her there several times. How she wailed! Papa carried her inside where Mama smoothed baking soda on all the bites. All of an instant Sally stopped crying, that is how fast soda works. Mama said if it happens again when we're out in the field to use mud.

Tomorrow and Wednesday we will make our candles, enough to last through next winter. When I carry mine upstairs and look out a snowy window, I shall remember our soldiers. I shall remember to complain not about being cold or having unpleasant chores.

June 18, 1778, Thursday

Riders galloped through Valley Forge early this morning, crying out, "The British are leaving Philadelphia!"

Where they are going, Papa knows not. Moments later our soldiers began forming ranks. The generals are on horseback and we've seen Baron von Steuben riding next to General Washington. Tents outside camp are coming down as it is warm enough to sleep without shelter, and there is much shouting of orders and busyness.

June 19, 1778, Friday

We woke at five o'clock this morning to a drumbeat, a quickstep. We hurriedly dressed—Mama held Johnny, Helen carried Olivia in her shawl—and we ran into the road. It was dark save for a few distant torches.

"The Army is leaving," said Papa. "God bless them and God bless America."

By noon the huts were deserted, the valley was quiet. We could see the camp followers straggling out with hand-carried belongings and a noisy assortment of children and dogs.

Papa rode into the encampment with Mr. Potter and Mr. Adams. "It is a mess," they said when they returned. "It shall take weeks to bury the garbage and dead animals."

Before Mrs. Hewes could move back into her house, Mama and us girls went to clean. What a sight. All I can say is there were many muddy boots that went in and out, and many chairs and tables that banged against the walls and scraped the floors. The entire house needs paint.

And I suspect Mrs. Hewes will be disappointed the officers used her parlour to powder their hair and wigs, for the walls are covered with white dust. (I think a respectable home should have its own little powder room with looking glass, combs, etc., for neatness' sake.)

Mrs. Adams brought two of her roosters to clean the chimneys. Her husband climbed onto the roof and into each cold chimney he dropped one of the birds. They flapped their wings frantically, brushing the stone insides until chunks of soot began raining down. After a few minutes they were so tired they dropped into the empty hearths. The birds did not die, but they looked like they wished to.

I suspect the Adamses will have roast chicken for supper tonight.

June 20, 1778, Saturday

A hush has fallen over the valley. I'd forgotten how quiet it used to be and how much I love the stillness.

Where the Army has marched we know not. Every meal Papa leads us in prayer for the safety of our soldiers and victory for General Washington.

Just before sunset a letter arrived for me. I quickly broke the seal. After reading, I did not throw it into the fire, but pasted it onto this page:

Dear Abigail,

I must tell you some surprising news . . .

Yesterday I visited the wigmaker, remember his tiny shop next door to Auntie Hannie? He said my hair was made into a beautiful wig for the wife of a general who wintered at Valley Forge. When I inquired "who is she?" he looked through his papers and showed me the order. Do you know, Abby, that the note was signed by Martha Washington herself? Now I can sleep again. Thank God my foolish mistake did not land my hair on the head of one of those plump British officers.

How I miss you, Abby, and my own family as well. I shall soon be home.

Your loving friend, Lucy

June 22, 1778, Monday

Papa has gone with the other men to reclaim their fences. All day they worked at tearing down huts and loading wagons with wood.

The children comb the grassy fields for musket balls to use for marbles. Mama says the flat ones she can make into buttons by drilling two holes in the center.

Elisabeth and I walked to the schoolhouse. It's being used still as a hospital, which pleases me. Everywhere we look are signs of fresh graves. Papa said nearly 3,000 soldiers died this winter and there was not even a battle.

At supper Papa poured each of us a toddy and held up his mug to toast. "To our new Army," he said. "Six months ago all we had was a bunch of volunteers from the 13 colonies and now look at them, ye saw them, girls. We have a real Continental Army now, ready to send the Redcoats back to King George, hip hooray! May God bless our every man."

June 23, 1778, Tuesday

The sun is hot.

I saw Elisabeth sitting under our big oak tree,

writing a letter against her knees. Her ink jug was burrowed in the dirt beside her so it wouldn't tip over.

I sat in the shade and leaned against the trunk so I could spy at her paper. She covered it with her hand, then turned to me with a laugh.

"Since thou must know, Little Sister, I am writing to Ben Valentine."

"Why?"

"Abby, he was kind and gentle, he appreciated my coat even though I had sewn it with selfish motives. I'm writing to tell him I shall pray every day for his safety and well-being. And when the war is over I shall cook him dinner."

I knew not what to think so I said something silly. "Well, then, why do thee not also write a letter to Azor?"

Elisabeth laughed again. "Oh, Abby."

June 26, 1778, Friday

This has been the hottest summer I remember. The nights are so steamy we sleep on cots outside, but the mosquitoes are vicious. They do not bother us if we stay in with the doors and windows fastened, but then the heat is so heavy we cannot sleep.

So Mama has taken to rubbing laurel leaves and mint on our faces, hands, and necks, and having us sleep in long-sleeved dresses with cotton leggings. This way we can lie on our cots and stare at the sky. The stars are so bright we can see the dark hillsides and the shadows of bats as they fly about. All night there is a faraway murmur from the creek.

I think about Mrs. Washington. Somehow I feel not so lonesome for her, knowing she may be wearing Lucy's beautiful brown hair. I'm beginning to believe that unpleasant events often work together for good, like a coat of many colors.

June 29, 1778, Monday

Criers rode through Valley Forge this morning with news of a battle yesterday near Monmouth Courthouse. While our Army fought the British, General Washington rode back and forth among the ranks of his soldiers until his horse dropped dead from exhaustion. At sunset both armies stopped fighting so they could rest, then after midnight the enemy snuck away.

We know not how many of our soldiers were wounded or killed, but we worry for them. They are like family to us now. Elisabeth must wait patiently for word about Ben Valentine.

I watch her wait and I puzzle how it has happened that strangers from last winter have become so dear.

June 30, 1778, Tuesday

More news about the Battle of Monmouth:

Three women stepped in to help with cannons after their husbands fainted from the heat. It has been the hottest June in memory and even some of the horses collapsed.

Other news pleased me: General Charles Lee was stripped of his command by General Washington, because he disobeyed orders and retreated in haste.

Papa said, "Bravo. The man is a coward, an embarrassment to the Patriots."

July 3, 1778, Friday

Much pie baking and visiting between the farms to borrow eggs, flour, sugar, bacon, and so-forth. We are all very much glad to replenish our larders and not worry about thieves, although if our soldiers should again be in need, I think I shall be one of the first to share.

Tomorrow is a celebration for Independence Day. It has been two years since the Declaration was signed and even though the British shant leave us alone, we shall still have a party!

Papa sawed our front and back doors in half, then re-hung them so we can latch the lower half. With the tops open we catch a breeze, but Johnny can't crawl out and no wild animals can crawl in.

July 4, 1778, Saturday

It is late and I am tired.

A breeze rose this afternoon that made the heat bearable. We are sleeping inside with windows open and the upper doors open. The breeze is pleasant and not allowing mosquitoes to land on us. I am dead sleepy, thus shall be brief.

Some of the soldiers' May Poles were still in camp, so much of the day we children played and ran around them, using rope to swing on. There are still many trinkets to be found in the grass and dirt, even enough cannon balls to play Long Bullet.

At noon, blankets were spread in the shade along the banks of the Schuylkill. A finer barbeque I've not enjoyed — Mr. and Mrs. Fitzgerald butchered two of their cows to share with everyone, so grateful they are for all our prayers and concern. There also were dozens of meat pies, fruit pies, and pumpkin pies passed around; cider and sweet lemonade, too.

Baby Olivia is nearly two months old and is quite content. No wonder. There is always someone wanting to hold her and kiss her. Johnny looks like a giant next to her. He now pulls himself up and with one hand on a tree trunk walks around it in a circle, around and around. He is sore proud of himself.

Colonel DeWees gave a patriotic speech, but I did not listen. It was hot and I wanted to play in the stream.

Tomorrow I shall have to ask Mama for more paper to sew together, so I can keep writing my journal . . . I want to record every word we hear about our Army. Papa says the war might continue many more months, but he's not worried. He has so much confidence in General Washington and our newly trained soldiers, that he says we shall beat the British for sure.

The crickets are loud tonight! And there is an owl nesting in our barn. When he flies out to do his night hunting he passes our window, his wings like a whisper

One more thought before I blow out my candle. I do hope Ben Valentine receives Elisabeth's letter.

Epilogue

During the Battle of Monmouth, Ben Valentine was shot in the left wrist. His arm was amputated on the field, then he was sent to Philadelphia to recover. Over the weeks, Elisabeth visited him, a romance developed, and they were married in the summer of 1779.

Two summers later, at the age of 15, Abigail married a blacksmith named Willie Campbell. Another wedding took place at this time: The young widow, Helen Kern, married Daniel Kern, her deceased husband's brother, so she remained "Mrs. Kern." They eventually had five children together.

In 1787 the Valentines and Campbells, the Stewarts and Kerns, moved west to homestead in the Ohio River Valley.

Abigail and Willie had nine children. Their daughter, Hannah, became the first woman doctor in Philip's County, and three sons became lawyers; one moved to Washington City to be President Thomas Jefferson's personal counsel.

Abigail died in 1823 at the age of 57, after being

thrown from her horse. Willie died two years later . . . some say from grief.

Elisabeth and Ben had four daughters who died in infancy, but their sons, Paul and Nathaniel, grew up to be explorers. Paul helped map the Missouri River and its surrounding territory. He was good friends with Daniel Boone.

At the age of 13, Nathaniel ventured to Boston and signed on as a cabin boy aboard the ship Otter, captained by the legendary China trader Ebenezer Dorr, Jr. They sailed into Monterey Bay in October of 1796, the first American vessel to anchor in a California port.

Elisabeth and Ben died together when their house caught fire in 1825.

Life in
America
in 1777

Historical Note

The American Revolution, also known as the War for Independence, was fought between 1775 and 1783. For the first time in history, the thirteen American colonies banded together as a nation so that they could fight against Britain and achieve their own independence. Over the years, Britain and their ruler, King George III, had given the colonies a lot of freedom to govern themselves by allowing each colony to have its own legislature. In return, the colonies were given the protection of the British Empire and its famous Royal Navy.

But then, in 1764, Britain imposed the Sugar Act and, a year later, the Stamp Act on the colonies. These acts forced Americans to pay very high taxes on sugar, legal documents, newspapers, and other items being imported into the colonies. Since the colonies had not been consulted about this, there were many riots and protests. This was "taxation without representation," and the colonists had no intention of cooperating. In 1767, Britain's Parliament passed the Townshend Acts, which placed outrageously high taxes on items such as paper, glass, paint, and tea.

The colonists continued to protest and tried to boycott British products. Finally, in late 1773, some rebellious citizens in Boston crept onto a British supply ship in Boston Harbor. They found more than three hundred chests of tea and dumped them into the water. Britain was furious about this and began to pass even more punitive laws, which the colonists described as the Intolerable Acts.

For many years the colonies had acted like thirteen little countries, but now it was time to work together. In 1774, the First Continental Congress met in Philadelphia, with representatives from twelve of the thirteen colonies. They agreed to remain under British authority, but decided that they wanted the right to create their own laws and taxes, without British interference. They also agreed to ban most imported products from Britain. Britain's response to this was to bring troops, the Redcoats, into the colonies. While the colonies had no army of their own, small local volunteer groups began to form militias, so that they would be able to defend themselves.

Then, one night in April 1775, British troops

were ordered to march from Boston out to Concord, Massachusetts, where they were planning to arrest rebel leaders and seize weapons and ammunition. That was the night Paul Revere crossed Boston Harbor and took his famous ride on horseback through the nearby towns, shouting a warning to one and all. When the Redcoats arrived in Lexington, the rebels — also known as the "patriots" — were there to greet them.

Nobody knows who fired that first shot, but it is called "the shot heard 'round the world." The rebels ended up chasing the Redcoats all the way back to Boston. Considering how many thousands of shots were fired that day, surprisingly few people were killed, but the war had now begun.

A few weeks later the Second Continental Congress met and decided to form a Continental Army. They selected a man who had been a great hero in the French and Indian War to be their general. His name was George Washington. He had never run an army before, but he turned out to be a born leader.

Early in 1776, a writer named Thomas Paine published a pamphlet titled *Common Sense*. In it, Paine described the terrible tyranny King George III was forcing on the colonies and called for complete independence. The Continental Congress agreed. They appointed a small committee to draft some resolutions for the colonies, now to be described as "states." Three of the five men on the committee were Thomas Jefferson, Benjamin Franklin, and John Adams. It was primarily Jefferson who wrote a document called the Declaration of Independence, and the Congress voted it into law on July 4, 1776.

There seemed to be very little chance that these tiny united states could defeat the great British Empire. Britain had a population of eight million people, a thriving economy, and the finest naval and armed forces in the world. The total population in the colonies was only two and a half million, and half a million of these citizens were still pledging allegiance to King George. They were called "loyalists" or "Tories," and they refused to help the patriots in the war against Britain. There were also half a million slaves, who were not allowed to fight, and two hundred thousand more people who were "neutralists" and would not fight at all. The colonies were not only outnumbered, but they also had no army, no navy, and almost no factories to manufacture the weapons and other supplies they would need. The only advantage they did have was that Britain was three thousand miles away, across the Atlantic Ocean, and would have a hard time supplying its own troops.

Britain's goal in the war was to squash the rebellion and force the colonies back under British rule, while America's goal was to gain total freedom and independence. The first major skirmish was the Battle of Bunker Hill—which actually took place on nearby Breed's Hill, in Boston. Neither side won. The British should have easily defeated the small amateur militia but, because the undermanned patriots fought so well, the British knew they were in for a difficult fight.

The British decided that if they could capture New York and the Hudson River, they could cut the colonies in half. During the lengthy Battle of Long Island, British General Sir William Howe almost managed to do just that. He was able to chase General Washington and his untrained soldiers from Brooklyn Heights all the way to Pennsylvania and probably could have defeated the colonists once and for all. But wars were fought very differently in the 1700s and, among other things, most armies took the winter off. Transportation was difficult under any circumstances, and the cold winter months made fighting almost impossible.

Having succeeded sufficiently for the time being, Howe withdrew back to New York. However, while Howe's army was resting and the general was busy going to parties and enjoying his holiday season, George Washington led his troops on a sneak Christmas attack. Washington and his militia crossed the Delaware River in boats, surrounded the British fort in Trenton, New Jersey, and forced the one thousand soldiers inside to surrender. Washington and his troops escaped before General Howe's army could retaliate.

The war continued in small, indecisive battles during 1777. The British were able to capture Philadelphia and won large battles at Fort Ticonderoga and Fort Edward in New York. But only a few weeks later, the Americans forced over 5,000 British soldiers to surrender at Saratoga. It was the first genuine victory for the United States and the turning point of the war. France, which had remained neutral, now decided that the United States would ultimately prevail, and the French agreed to become an ally. Throughout the rest of the war, the French were often able to provide desperately needed supplies and financial assistance to the colonists. Without this help, the Americans might not have been able to hang on long enough to win the war.

The winter of 1777–1778 is famous because Washington brought his troops to Valley Forge, Pennsylvania, for the winter. Food and clothing were so scarce that as many as 4,000 soldiers—about a third of the army—were barefoot and starving. While this could have permanently destroyed the soldiers' willpower, these struggles ended up making them stronger. The troops spent the long, cold months being drilled and trained in military tactics. By the time spring arrived, the motley Continental Army had become a group of skilled professional soldiers.

The war continued on for the next several years. Britain couldn't manage to win, and the Americans would not give up. Finally, in late 1781, with France's help, America won a crucial victory at Yorktown, Virginia. They defeated British General Cornwallis, who was forced to surrender his entire British Army of 8,000 men. It was the last real battle of the war.

The next spring, peace talks began in Paris. Britain officially agreed to grant America its permanent independence and to withdraw all of its remaining troops from the country. America's victory was complete, and the Treaty of Paris was approved by the Continental Congress on April 15, 1783, and signed in September. It was almost exactly eight years after "the shot heard 'round the world," and the thirteen colonies had finally become a free and independent nation, the United States of America.

Typical dress of an eighteenth-century man. The tailored coat buttoned to the waist and then curved away to allow for freedom of movement.

Eighteenth-century women often wore shawls to fill in the low necklines of their gowns. Aprons were considered fashionable decorations, and caps or bonnets were also popular.

The main room in an eighteenth-century home, where the family cooked, ate, and worked. The fireplace provided some warmth, but the houses were still quite cold during the winter.

171

THE
SCHOOL
OF
MANNERS.
OR
RULES for Childrens
Behaviour:

AtChurch,at Home,atTable,
inCompany,inDiscourse,at
School,abroad, and among
Boys. With some other
short and mixt Precepts.

By the Author of the *English
Exercises.*

The Fourth Edition.

LONDON.
Printed for *Tho. Cockerill,* at the
ThreeLegs andBible against Gro-
cers-Hall in the *Poultrey,* 1701.

Teaching manners to children was very important in Colonial America. Many books contained rules of courtesy and behavior, such as The School of Manners, *first published in London in 1701.*

An excerpt from The School of Manners. *The rules for etiquette are borrowed from a famous earlier book called* Youths' Behaviour, or Decency in Conversation Amongst Men. *Note that S's look like F's.*

17. Bite not thy bread, but break it, but not with slovenly Fingers, nor with the same wherewith thou takest up thy meat,

18 Dip not thy Meat in the Sawce.

19. Take not salt with a greasy Knife.

20 Spit not, cough not, nor blow thy Nose at Table if it may be avoided; but if there be necessity, do it aside, and without much noise.

21. Lean not thy Elbow on the Table, or on the back of thy Chair.

22. Stuff not thy mouth so as to fill thy Cheeks; be content with smaller Mouthfuls.

23. Blow not thy Meat, but with Patience wait till it be cool,

24. Sup not Broth at the Table, but eat It with a Spoon.

Charles Willson Peale was one of the most famous portrait painters of the eighteenth century. He painted some of the best-known portraits of George Washington, such as the one from which the illustration shown here is drawn. His son, Rembrandt Peale, painted this portrait of Martha Washington.

Martha Washington arrives in her carriage at Valley Forge.

The young American soldiers slept in tents until they could build log huts. Without proper shelter, enough food, or shoes, the troops were poorly prepared to fight the able British Army.

The British soldiers were outfitted in formal uniforms.

*Commander in Chief
George Washington
issued this request,
seeking aid for his men,
to all people in the
Valley Forge area.*

*Washington's
Headquarters in
Valley Forge.*

The Declaration of Independence, written primarily by Thomas Jefferson over the course of seventeen days, explains why Americans should fight for their freedom from the oppressive British king. "We hold these truths to be self-evident," it decrees, "that all men are created equal."

The Yankee's
RETURN FROM CAMP.

FATHER and I went down to camp,
　　Along with captain Gooding
There we see the men and boys,
　　As thick as hasty-pudding,
　　　　Yankee doodle keep it up,
　　　　Yankee doodle dandy;
Cho.— *Mind the Music and the step,*
　　　　And with the girls be handy.

And there we see a thousand men,
　　As rich as 'Squire David;
And what they wasted every day,
　　I wish it could be saved.
　　　　Yankee doodle, &c.

The 'lasses they eat every day,
　　Would keep an house a winter,
They have as much that I'll be bound,
　　They eat it when they're amind to,
　　　　Yankee doodle, &c.

And there we see a swamping gun,
　　Large as a log of maple,
Upon a duced little cart,
　　A load for father's cattle,
　　　　Yankee doodle, &c.

And every time they shoot it off,
　　It takes a horn of powder;
It makes a noise like father's gun,
　　Only a nation louder.
　　　　Yankee doodle, &c.

I went as nigh to one myself,
　　As 'Siah's under-pinning;
And father went as nigh again,
　　I thought the duce was in him.
　　　　Yankee doodle, &c.

Cousin Simon grew so bold,
　　I thought he would have cock'd it;
It scar'd me so I streak'd it off,
　　And hung by father's pocket.
　　　　Yankee doodle, &c.

But Captain Davis has a gun,
　　He kind of clap'd his hand on't,
And stuck a crooked stabbing iron,
　　Upon the little end on't.
　　　　Yankee doodle, &c.

And there I see a pumpkin shell,
　　As big as mother's bason,
And every time they touch'd it off,
　　They scamper'd like the nation.
　　　　Yankee doodle, &c.

I see a little barrel too,
　　The heads were made of leather,
They knock'd upon it with little clubs,
　　And call'd the folks together,
　　　　Yankee doodle, &c.

And there was Captain Washington,
　　And gentlefolks about him,
They say he's grown so tarnal proud,
　　He will not ride without 'em.
　　　　Yankee doodle, &c.

He got him on his meeting clothes,
　　Upon a slapping stallion,
He set the world along in rows,
　　In hundreds and in millions.
　　　　Yankee doodle, &c.

The flaming ribbons in their hats,
　　They look'd so tearing fine, ah,
I wanted plaguily to get,
　　To give to my Jemima.
　　　　Yankee doodle, &c.

I see another snarl of men,
　　A digging graves, they told me,
So tarnal long, so tarnal deep,
　　They 'tended they should hold me.
　　　　Yankee doodle, &c.

It scar'd me so, I hook'd it off,
　　Nor stopp'd as I remember,
Nor turn'd about till I got home,
　　Lock'd up in mother's chamber.
　　　　Yankee doodle, &c.

Sold, wholesale and retail, at 132, Ann Street, Boston.

Lyrics to an early version of the popular song "Yankee Doodle." The expression Yankee Doodle, coined by the British soldiers, was meant to mock the young American army. But it quickly became the Americans' rallying cry — and their theme song.

177

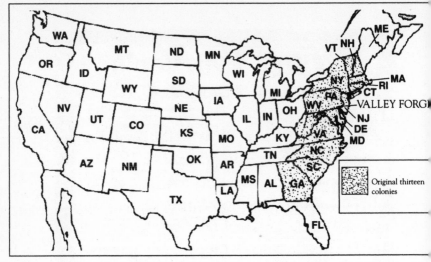

Modern map of the continental United States, showing the approximate location of Valley Forge, and the original thirteen colonies.

This detail of Valley Forge and its outlying areas shows important places and battles sites of the American Revolution.

About the Author

KRISTIANA GREGORY is well-known for her accurate and compelling historical fiction for middle-grade and young adult readers, bringing the adventures and struggles of young people during many different times in American history vividly to life. The Revolutionary War period has always held a particular personal interest for her.

"I've always felt a kinship with this period of history because many of my ancestors fought in the Revolutionary War, including one who was camped at Valley Forge during the winter of 1777–1778. His name was William Kern, and he was a sergeant in Daniel Morgan's 11th Virginia Regiment.

"One of my visits to Valley Forge was on a Christmas Day. It was bitterly cold and the snow was knee-deep. Shivering, I peered inside one of the log huts and tried to imagine the poor soldiers without shoes or warm clothes. It fascinated me to realize that George Washington had ridden his horse along that very road. My ancestor may have spoken to him."

Writing *The Winter of Red Snow* allowed her to imagine what it really would have been like to watch the young American soldiers prepare for war and also to experience the excitement of meeting George Washington. And though the diary is a work of fiction, most of the events and characters are real, including von Steuben's 17-year-old interpreter, Pierre Etienne Duponceau, and his polite greyhound, Azor, as well as George Washington's expense account, which records a payment of "40 shillings a month, plus 4 shillings per dozen pieces" to a laundress named Peggy Lee.

Ms. Gregory discovered that, "After the war, William Kern's brother, Adam, married a young woman named Christiana, coincidentally my namesake."

Ms. Gregory's historical fiction novels include *Jimmy Spoon and the Pony Express* and *The Stowaway*, as well as *Clementine*, *Jenny of the Tetons*, *The Legend of Jimmy Spoon*, and *Earthquake at Dawn*. She lives in Idaho with her family.

Acknowledgments

I'm deeply grateful to Pennsylvanians Betty Page of the Valley Forge Historical Society and Elsie Mullin, for their help with research.

The recipe of "Martha Washington's Great Cake" was provided by The Women's Committee of the Valley Forge Historical Society, Valley Forge, Pennsylvania.

Grateful acknowledgment is made for permission to use the following:

Cover portrait by Tim O'Brien.

Cover background: *Washington's Headquarters—Valley Forge.* Watercolor painting by Roland Lee, www. rolandlee.com. Used with permission.

Page 171 (top): *Everyday Dress of Rural America,* Dover Publications, Inc., New York.

Page 171 (bottom): *A New England Kitchen,* Art Resource, New York.

Page 172 (top): Title page from *The School of Manners, or Rules for Children's Behaviour,* John Garretson, London: Oregon Press for the Victoria and Albert Museum, 1701, 1983.

Page 172 (bottom): Excerpt from *The School of Manners,* ibid.

Page 173 (top): Illustration of George Washington after a portrait by Charles Willson Peale, *The American Revolution: A Picture Sourcebook,* Dover Publications, Inc., New York.

Page 173 (top): *Martha Washington* by Rembrandt Peale, © The Metropolitan Museum of Art/Art Resource, NY.

Page 173 (bottom): *Martha Washington Arrives at Valley Forge* by Henry Alexander Ogden. Collection of The New-York Historical Society, 1936. 850.

Page 174 (top): *Washington and Lafayette at Valley Forge,* Culver Pictures, Inc.

Page 174 (bottom): British soldier's uniform, *The American Revolution: A Picture Sourcebook,* Dover Publications, Inc., New York.

Page 175 (top) George Washington's request, ibid.

Page 175 (bottom): *Washington's Headquarters at Valley Forge* by Henry Alexander Ogden. Collection of The New-York Historical Society, 1936. 849.

Page 176: Declaration of Independence, The National Archives.

Page 177: "The Yankee's Return from Camp," *The American Revolution: A Picture Sourcebook*, Dover Publications, Inc., New York.

Page 178: Maps by Heather Saunders.

Other books in the
Dear America series